The Scientific Method

by Joey W. Hill

Acknowledgments

My great thanks to Helen and Gina, my science advisors. I am not a science person at all, so their assistance was invaluable to better reflect the world and thought processes so familiar to Brian and Debra. My gratitude also goes out to Mindy for coming to my rescue during the "erotic anatomy lesson" – love you, darling! My additional fervent thanks to Erin for her proofing abilities. Back-to-back edits fried my brain, such that I desperately needed another set of eyes in the three days before deadline. She came to the plate and delivered wonderfully.

Any remaining shortcomings are entirely the fault of this author, who hopes you enjoy Brian and Debra regardless. Hugs to everyone who has waited for their story for so long. I hope I did it justice!

Author's Note: While this book is a novella of the Vampire Queen series, happening somewhere after the time frame of Book VIII, *Bound by the Vampire Queen*, it can be read as a standalone. However, a familiarity with my vampire world will certainly enhance your enjoyment. You can read blurbs and excerpts for all the books in this series at http://www.storywitch.com/series-vqs.

Chapter One

Debra. I'm hungry.

Two words that always meant something much more than blood to vampires.

She found him in Lady Lyssa's gardens. The old stone bench under an arbor weighted down by Confederate jasmine was his favored place to work when he didn't have to be in the lab. He was studying his laptop now, which provided her time to look at him as she approached.

The moonlight limned his hair, giving the lighter strands a golden-silver luster. The sculpted planes of his face were etched by shadow. With the preternatural vampire stillness that could take him when he was deep in thought, he could have been another marble statue in the maze of gardens.

Though he often came out of his work as if emerging from the bottom of a still ocean, she felt the moment his focus sharpened on her. It was a transition that never failed to weaken her knees. The awareness in his eyes, a mixture of blood hunger, sexual need and…

No, that was all there was. That was all she could let herself think about. For her part, it was so much more, but that was her problem to handle. She was the human in the relationship. A servant to his needs.

Setting aside his laptop, he brought her between his knees, banded his arms around her and nuzzled her throat. No words. They didn't need them, did they? She wound her arms around his shoulders, taking advantage of those first few seconds to slide her fingers through his thick hair, her pulse tripping as he slipped the buttons of her blouse and licked the valley between her breasts, tracing the curves. The man could use his tongue, the way a master painter used a fine brush. The pressure, stroke, timing… Totally controlled and excruciatingly perfect.

If a vampire wanted to fuck his servant in plain view of everyone on the Council estate, no one thought a thing about it. But right now, they were blissfully alone. Brian slid a hand up under her skirt to cup her buttock. When he found his way beneath her panties to stimulate her rim with long fingers, she moaned, rubbing her mound against his chest. The look he lifted to her was full of heat and pleasure, reflecting that dangerous edge that left no doubt—at least in this moment—that he considered her totally his.

His other hand slid along the curve of her breast, up to her throat, stroking so she lifted her chin, drawing in her breath at the whisper of his own there, the brush of his fangs. Those vibrant hazel eyes watched her every reaction.

"Stay still," he said, and she didn't move a muscle, even though inside all of her nerve endings were dancing. He pressed his mouth against her throat again and, as his fangs penetrated, he slowly slid his fingers into her wet pussy.

Clasp your hands behind your back. He spoke to her mind to mind, but it didn't lessen the command. When she obeyed, the thrust of her breasts put her tight nipples against his upper chest, an excruciating friction.

My bad girl. Already so hot and wet. You're going to come without my permission.

No, my lord.

You're saying no to me?

He took a particular delight in befuddling her usually organized mind like that. She could tell it in the gleam of his gaze, the erotic set of his irresistible mouth as he briefly lifted his head, gave her a look. She gave a desperate half laugh. "No, my lord. I mean, yes. Oh…"

He scissored and thrust his fingers in a rhythm with his drinking that elicited tiny moans, made her lose her train of thought.

You're going to come for me.

"Yes." She breathed it, shut her eyes and pressed her jaw against his head as the climax rose up inside her, an irresistible wave. She'd do anything for him.

He locked his arm around her, holding her fast so her sensual writhings worked her against his body. As he took his nourishment from her throat again, he kept stroking and teasing her until she wanted nothing more than to grip his shoulders, hold on forever.

But she wasn't allowed to touch him until he said she could.

§

That had been a couple hours before dawn, quite a few hours ago, but her body still vibrated with need. Debra opened her eyes, staring at rows of clean test tubes, mounted in the stainless steel drying rack on the wall across from her. The light thrown in from the west window gleamed off the glass. The rack kept them equidistant, allowing them to dry evenly and completely. Such order usually soothed her, centering her mind, but today she had an absurd urge to make the tubes fall. Make them touch, shatter against one another. Their rigid order felt like a mockery, a flimsy screen over a world making less and less sense to her.

She knew recalling her Master's latest feeding was a double-edged form of self-comfort, but it didn't stop her from recalling every ounce of sensory input. His hair against her skin. The thick strands scattered over his forehead and brushing his collar were the color of sunbaked golden sand, mixed with the darker bronze of it close to the shoreline. He'd had a scattering of Confederate jasmine blooms on his shoulders. Then there was his scent. The sharp cleanliness of the lab had been integrated with the smell of cut grass and old stone.

She thought of his eyes, focused and sharp. His firm mouth, commanding her to sink to her trembling knees after her climax and his feeding. He'd unbuckled the belt of his slacks, opened them to reach in and grip his steel length. He'd stretched his cock out over the snug fit of his underwear, fed it between her parted lips, her moan of eagerness to serve him vibrating against the broad head.

In the vampire world, Lord Brian might be thought unassuming because he was more interested in gaining scientific knowledge than political power, but the inherent Dominant nature all vampires carried was just as full-blown in him as in a member of the Vampire Council.

Unfortunately, it tended to show itself only in short bursts; during feedings or at social events. If he was present for the event, that is. All too often he sent Debra by herself, because it was required that a lower-ranking vampire would make his servant available for such formal occasions. Here on Lady Lyssa's estate, where high-ranking vampires regularly came to petition the Council, most vampires wouldn't get away with sending their servant but not making an appearance themselves. However, if Brian wasn't there, he was in the research wing of the estate, his quarters, or the gardens, his brilliant mind employed with vital issues that affected the wellbeing of vampire kind.

Performing sexual acts with other servants for the pleasure of watching vampires was part of being in their very carnal world. She'd learned to embrace the sensuality of it, realizing she was honoring her Master by performing well, handling those things so he could spend time on his work. Even so, being at those events without him was never easy. She was indebted to the kindness of other servants who'd helped her grow more comfortable with it. By going to a place in her mind where she imagined him in the group of watching vampires, speaking in her head, ordering her every move, she could sometimes even make it pleasurable.

Since Lady Lyssa had taken over the Council leadership, she'd pretty much excused Debra from any formal vampire dinner requirements if Brian wasn't going to be present. It was a significant change from when the Council had been under Belizar's leadership. Though she suspected Jacob, Lyssa's servant, had been behind that decision, Debra was grateful for it.

When she'd met Brian at the university-affiliated research facility where she was working, he'd recognized she was a bone-deep submissive, one who had never articulated her needs. Instead, she'd channeled all of it into who she was as a scientist, serving the greater good, always asking more of herself, pushing harder. The bar was always rising, every breakthrough only a step toward the next one. She was an extreme overachiever with a dazzling mind, responsible for the acquisition of several key grants for the facility and, despite her age, in line for a fellowship.

Yet after only a short period of time in Brian's company, she'd left the world of human research and committed her life to him as his third marked servant. For one thing, he'd offered her an incomparable professional opportunity. She managed the day-to-day operations of the multiple wings of the research facility here at the Council headquarters. That also included management of the human staff of sixteen second marked servants who worked in those wings.

Working side by side with Brian, they'd made outstanding breakthroughs on the Delilah virus and vampire fertility issues that had made a difference to the species as a whole. Some of those breakthroughs had led to discoveries related to human disease. She'd forwarded those findings to a trusted contact at her old research facility and allowed her to take the credit, Debra remaining anonymous. Which was fine. The real reward was working with Brian himself.

The way her and Brian's minds meshed when they solved problems created a synergy so profound, it was no different from the exhilaration of shooting down the water slide in the amusement park of her youth.

She hadn't wanted to go to that amusement park, but her grandfather had said she was too serious, that she needed to get out and live life as much as study it. When she hit the pool at the bottom of the slide, the rush of the water, the pleasure of turning somersaults and getting a buoyant sense of herself different from what she'd ever known, had in fact been liberating. It made her a better scientist.

Her grandfather had taught her to seek different ways of looking at things. *There's always one perfect angle to see everything that's important. But remember the sun shines on a different world every day. Getting trapped into one way of thinking is quicksand.*

She could tell herself she'd left her old life for the science, but when Brian had unlocked the sexual side of her submission, he'd shown her it went down to her soul. When he held her, looked at her like he had in the garden, that was the perfect angle. It was the key to everything she needed from him and wanted to be for him. He was her Master, that one word the beginning and end of all of it. Which explained not only the main reason she'd followed him into his world, but why she was still with him, even during times like these, when the emptiness of her soul ached to be filled by things he could never offer her.

She glanced down at her tablet. The email she'd received several days ago was only a couple of taps away, but she already knew it by heart. Reading it again didn't change anything. Lack of change was the real problem, wasn't it?

A crackling noise penetrated her brooding, making her snap her attention to the left side of her desk. Emilie was chewing on her pencil like a beaver taking down a tree.

"Emilie, no. You know better than that." Debra extricated the item from the tiny claws of the white mouse and offered her a pinch of sunflowers from the jar on her desk. The mouse sat up on her haunches, seed clasped in both paws as she nibbled with a satisfied air. Debra raised a brow.

"Think you have me trained like Pavlov's dog, don't you?" She took a pinch of seeds herself, chewed while she looked back down at her notes. They were complete; she knew they were. She should move on to the latest data reports about the Delilah virus, but instead she tapped the tab on her tablet marked "birthing data".

Everything they'd collected about vampire birth data was in there, from Kane, Lady Lyssa and Jacob's son, to the most recent pregnancy in the vampire world, the daughter born to Lord Mason and his servant Jessica. But Debra wasn't interested in reviewing statistics. Instead she chose Brian's formal presentation to the Vampire Council a few months ago. If she kept it in hardcopy, it would be like a worn love letter. A simple fact, not sentiment, and a scientist never discarded fact because it was too uncomfortable to face, did she?

What I have found is this: there is an undeniable connection between fertility and those vampires and servants who have a closer relationship than is considered acceptable in our world...

What they'd done was analyze a number of carefully selected factors from both fertile and non-fertile relationships, and the results overwhelmingly supported their theory. Each fertile test couple exhibited a higher level of intimacy and trust than their non-fertile counterpart, as well as some level of what they'd decided to label as "positive dependence".

Debra went back to the report, where they'd couched it in lay terms. Terms so potent she couldn't stop re-reading them.

Positive, in that the vampire still clearly held the dominant role in the relationship, but he or she valued the servant in a manner that strongly suggests an emotional bond. One that could be defined as deep, romantic love.

Servants could be valued confidantes, a constant blood source, useful for performing daylight chores. But they were still considered an inferior race. The idea that vampires could be in love with their servants, that there was some sort of emotional parity to the relationship? Taboo, to say the least. The specifics of these results had been kept confidential at the Council level, only a carefully edited summary allowed distribution to Region Masters and overlords. The Council needed time to digest the implications before they would be comfortable handling the reaction of the vampire world as a whole.

Deep, romantic love. She and Brian had debated the correct terminology to use for the presentation, and in the end agreed it would be best to go with a subjective term a layperson would understand, to maximize the impact. This wasn't about achieving rights for servants. Beyond having their existence publicly exposed to humans, born vampires faced no greater threat than the extraordinarily low birth rate. Made vampires for the most part simply didn't have the same longevity or strength. This was a significant finding, if the data continued to support it, and so far it had.

Closing her eyes, Debra remembered what else Brian had said to Lady Lyssa during that pivotal meeting. "I credit my lab assistant and servant with this finding. She pointed out the variable to me and backed it up."

It was ironic that when she'd met Lady Lyssa's servant, Jacob, Debra had been the one to give him the stern lecture about the nature of the relationship between vampires and servants. *The bond between servant and vampire is unique. Not family, not spouses, not lover. The excess sex drive vampires have can force us into a deceptive intimacy. We convince ourselves we're lovers, probably because the reality is beyond our ken and we don't know how to classify it. Since we can't reconcile the feeling with the reality, we use sex to Band-Aid it… If you allow yourself to believe it's something different from what it is, you've fooled yourself in a way that will only bring you heartbreak. In the worst cases it'll result in bitterness. They'll drive that lesson home again and again, twisting the knife.*

She'd been on the receiving end of that knife during her first couple of years as Brian's full servant. She considered herself a rational empiricist, so once she'd pushed past the emotional pain of what had happened, she'd analyzed it from all angles and accepted what her relationship to Brian could and couldn't be.

Or so she thought. Lately, things had been changing, new variables altering her ability to manage her feelings.

Lady Lyssa and Jacob had defied hundreds of years of strict vampire protocol on vampire-servant relationships. They were clearly a man and woman in love, no matter that as her servant Jacob only had the rights Lyssa gave to him. But what vampire law said and what people's hearts dictated were frequently different.

When Debra was around Jacob, it was clear how often Lyssa floated in and out of his mind. His handsome mouth would quirk, his eyes soften, brief flashes of humor crossing his features. Along with occasional wry frustration, since the last queen of the Far East clan was far from the most easy-going of vampires—an uncommon trait in any vampire, let alone one over a thousand years old with royal blood in her veins.

Though all third marked servants were linked to the minds of their vampires, Brian didn't spend much time in Debra's, not nearly as much as many other vampires did with their servants. Except when they were working. During those times, bringing together theory, hypotheses and testing across the bridge of their minds was so intense it was almost like lovemaking.

Sex, she corrected herself, setting her jaw. When they weren't working—or in the throes of sexual relations—her thoughts were her own. She should consider that a blessing, because plenty of servants grumbled about privacy being the major drawback of becoming a vampire's fully marked servant, the servant's mind unable to be shielded from the vampire's in any way, all the way down to the soul.

Brian had never shown much interest in that. What would it feel like, to have him reach out to her during his waking hours, touch her mind, her heart and soul? Know he was listening to her subconscious flow of thoughts and feelings for no other reason than he wanted to take advantage of that mind-to-mind bond he had with no other.

A scientist couldn't ask for more than what she had in this state-of-the-art facility, the work she was doing. Yet the main yearning she had in her life wasn't professional at all. It all revolved around an amazing vampire scientist from whom she wanted more than she could have.

She sighed, propped her chin on her hand. Damn it, she was supposed to be past all this ridiculous starry-eyed…bullshit. Way past. What was the matter with her?

Yet if she hadn't allowed for a variable as subjective as the depth of a relationship, she might never have found the connection between it and the fertility rate. So she knew the vulnerability of her heart contributed to her science. Even so, lately she wished she was as emotionless as a Vulcan.

Despite her morose thoughts, the thought gave her a tiny smile. Brian had every Star Trek series and movie made to date. His mind tended to run like a race car's RPM, so he occasionally put one in the player before dawn. At eighty-five, a young age for vampires, he couldn't stay awake more than an hour past sunrise, even in his bedroom below ground, but he said the space opera helped him sleep better.

When he watched the programs, he was different, less guarded.

Early in their relationship, she'd often spent the hour before dawn watching them with him. Curled up in bed together, sweat from their intense erotic encounters drying on her tingling flesh, she'd teased him, called him a geek.

Then she'd asked him if he loved her. That had ended the comfortable intimacy between them outside the lab.

"You don't look happy."

She glanced up to see Jacob leaning in the door frame. The highest-ranking servant in the vampire world didn't dress the part, wearing his Dragon Ale Tavern T-shirt and faded jeans. Given how well the cotton stretched and denim molded his muscular form, she didn't think anyone would object. Like vampires themselves, most servants were absurdly attractive, but there was an intelligence and charisma to Jacob that made it clear why the broad-shouldered, russet-haired male was such a good match for Lady Lyssa.

Brian's main research facility had been relocated from Berlin to this vast property outside Savannah, Georgia. Since Lyssa resided here at least part of the year because this was also where the Council had its primary base of operations, Jacob was a frequent and welcome visitor to Debra's lab. She'd been a servant far longer, but he'd been the one who most helped her adapt to vampire social events, the all-too-public sexual demands they placed on servants. Beyond that, he'd become a good friend. Perhaps her best friend, after Brian. Though thinking of her vampire Master as her friend was probably more evidence of her confused state of mind today.

"I'm fine," she said automatically. Jacob smelled like cookies, which told her the cook had been baking. It was too much to hope he'd brought her some. She thought of cookies baking in her grandmother's oven, the tremendous comfort and wealth of memory a single smell could contain, and that wave of sadness hit her again.

You can't do anything about it, she told herself. *Put it away.*

Jacob straddled a stool near the door, pushing off so he rolled across the floor to her, bumping into her to stop. Giving him a mock scowl, she bumped him back. "You're invading my space."

"I have sugar." He produced a small container of cookies, the lid cracked to release oven-baked heat.

He had thought to bring her some. Then again, she was dealing with Jacob, not Brian. Jacob anticipated a woman's needs.

Stop it. It's not your Master's job to even think about your needs. She admonished herself firmly, even as her heart twisted at the simple kindness of a friend.

"You're evil. And wonderful." She leaned in, gave his shoulder an exaggerated sniff. "Are you sure that smell isn't you, though? According to that giggling entourage of second marks with Lady Helga last week, you are cookies, chocolate and a foot massage all rolled up into one."

"Can't help that I'm irresistible." He shrugged, fending off her shove.

Emilie was so used to him, she didn't even bother to look up from her seeds. She'd been joined by her two brothers, Albert and Nicolai, scampering out of their open cage. Debra's work desk in the corner was one of the few things she'd brought from her old life. Engraved with famous equations, symbols and sayings of historic thinkers, the polished heavy oak surface looked like it would be at home in a ship.

To remind you that science is a voyage, not a destination, her grandfather had said. He'd made it for her. Her desk was the only place in the lab the mice were allowed to be out of their cage, mounted above the corner. They had a short, colorful set of Lego steps descending from the open door to help them reach the desk surface. Jacob nodded. "That's a new renovation."

"Courtesy of your son and his constant shadow, John."

Jacob smiled at that, touched Emilie's silky back with one gentle finger. "I see Whiskers has successfully been kept clear of the lab, else you'd be down three mice."

"I threatened to declaw and defang her last time she was here. She hasn't been back."

"You're as gentle as you can be with animals. I don't believe it." He cocked a brow at her, those shrewd eyes measuring. "You know, you're always way too serious, but serious and unhappy are different things. So what's up?"

When she didn't immediately reply, he tugged her stool closer, sliding an arm around her. The strength of his body and his scent—which really did seem to have something magnetic to female senses—was a balm to her, not a sexual enticement, but that was part of their friendship as well.

Since servants were often required to perform sexually together during vampire gatherings, she and Jacob had been down that road. But it was part of their service to their Master and Mistress, respectively. Jacob would never dream of touching Debra sexually except under Lyssa's command, so his generous physical affection in a platonic context was a comfort she could never resist, because Brian rarely did casual affection anymore. Jacob also understood how she felt about Brian. It was okay for servants to love their Masters, after all. Just not in reverse. No matter what that study said. One conclusion didn't change centuries of embedded class culture.

Damn it, damn it, damn it. She pushed away from Jacob, earning a startled look. "It's not you. I'm sorry, Jacob. I'm working on a particularly frustrating issue today and it's gotten under my skin. Just ignore me. Come back tomorrow and I'll be in a better mood."

Instead of leaving, he rose and laid his hands on her shoulders. "Debra."

"It's nothing." Her half-laugh fell short of humor and landed right into despair territory. "The servant version of the seven year itch. You look down the road, and you realize the relationship won't ever change, but this is the relationship I signed up for. With eyes wide open. It's a phase. I'm sure plenty of servants have gone through it."

She was staring at Jacob's chest, using her finger to draw equations on it, something she did to calm a racing mind. Her lungs were drawing in far too little air. His hands kneaded her shoulders. "Breathe," he murmured. "Psycho OCD nerd."

"Dumb jock."

"Not me. Gideon was the football star."

Jacob referred to his brother, Gideon Green, the former vampire hunter who was now unlikely servant to two vampires, Anwyn and Lord Daegan. "I was the Dungeons and Dragon kid," he added. "The one who talked my friends into tilting with lances on our bicycles. Shoving the lance in the spokes is a great way to unhorse your opponent."

"That's cheating. You're supposed to aim for the knight, not his horse."

He smiled. "Why am I not surprised you know that? You know everything."

She wished she knew everything. She wished she knew how to make her heart stop loving a man who'd made it clear he wouldn't love her back, even though they shared an intense relationship she could achieve with no one else.

Studying her face, Jacob drew her back to her chair, but instead of easing her onto it, he took it instead and put her on his lap, curving a hand over her hip to hold her in place, bounce her a little bit. It made her smile, as she was sure he intended. Emilie was at the edge of the desk, studying them. The mouse made a short leap, catching Jacob's shirt sleeve and using it to climb up to his shoulder and settle down under his hair, which was long enough to brush his shoulders.

When she sighed, unable to hold back her unhappiness, Jacob put both arms around her. He made it okay for her to put her head on his other shoulder. Using his long legs and the brace of his feet, he rocked the chair back and forth, back and forth. That was another thing about him. She didn't have to say anything, and he knew when not to talk. As well as when to do so, even if it made her uncomfortable.

"You remember what you told me that day in the library? About the limits of the vampire-servant relationship?"

"I was just thinking about that," she said.

He nodded, his jaw moving against her temple. Vampires had no facial hair, so it was only with other servants she experienced the rasp of beard shadow. Since Jacob shaved daily, it gave her an indication of the late afternoon hour, though she really didn't need it. From habit as well as an internal clock all third marks seemed to have, she knew when sundown was approaching. But Brian kept a small lab in his quarters. He might not appear until he needed the instruments in the main lab, was ready to check in with her on the day's work, or if he needed blood.

She shivered, remembering that last feeding again. Sexual attraction never diminished between vampire and servant, remaining intense and far too easy to confuse with emotions. She knew all the rational, chemical reasons for that. She should be able to manage it.

"You told me the first time you assumed your relationship with Brian was more than it could be for vampire and servant, the bastard took a female vampire in front of you."

"Jacob." Her cheeks colored. Even after all this time, it was a painful memory. When he was done, Brian had fed his cock into her mouth, still smelling of the other woman's cunt, and then he'd fucked Debra as well.

Yet long before that had happened, when she only had the first of the three marks necessary to become a vampire's full servant, Brian had grilled her with brutal thoroughness, made sure she understood exactly what the relationship between vampire and servant was like. She'd told him she understood. When her Master was 100% focused, nothing got past him. If she'd had an ounce of uncertainty, Brian would have let her go.

Then, two years into their relationship, she'd proven she hadn't learned the lesson well enough, and he'd reinforced it with that painful lesson. Though it had hurt like hell, she'd analyzed it, understood the message, and they'd moved on.

Even so, her body had stiffened. Jacob fished Emilie out of his hair and dumped her gently back on the counter. Then he moved to his stool and lowered Debra back into her chair to give her space, but he put his hand over hers, tangling fingers, his thumb moving over the top of her hand in an idle stroke.

"He needed to be horsewhipped for doing that. But the Lord Brian I've come to know these past few years isn't cruel without purpose, is he?" When she shook her head, he leaned back, crossing his arms over his chest. "Around that same time period, several servants were put to death in front of their vampires when it was ruled their Masters or Mistresses had become too attached to them. Brian's very good at detachment when he feels it's essential. It makes him capable of acts the rest of us might be too emotionally soft to pull off."

"He's a good man." On a normal day, she meant it. But her thought process today made her sound too wooden. Why couldn't facts affect her heart more than feelings?

"Yes, he is." Jacob studied her. "You've got a lot of his qualities, Debra. Sometimes I think your heart has to overflow before you'll let it have its say. Experiencing something like that—no matter his reasons for doing it—any woman would be afraid to let herself go back down that road again. However, Brian himself came to the conclusion, with your help, that a vampire-servant relationship can be more. Perhaps should be more."

No. Even as she rejected it, her kneejerk reaction told her how right Jacob was. Her heart clamped shut at the mere idea. It was bad enough to have it lurking around in her own mind, but to hear it voiced gave it even more strength, made it more dangerously irresistible.

"I'm just feeling vulnerable right now. There's nothing wrong with me and Brian. It's something else. My grandfather isn't well.

He's...dying." She laid her palm on the desk, traced one of the burned sets of letters. *The sun, with all those planets revolving around it and dependent on it, can still ripen a bunch of grapes as if it had nothing else in the universe to do. – Galileo*

Her grandfather had such a quirky, wonderful sense of humor. She took a breath. "My mother still emails me. I need to bring an end to that. I mean, we're going to outlive all of our family, aren't we? Except perhaps you and Gideon."

"As infuriating as Gideon is, that's not a foregone conclusion," Jacob said dryly. "Anwyn may put a railroad spike over his heart and let Daegan stomp it through his chest."

A reminder that metal through the heart took a servant's life. She wondered if that hurt less than heartache, but then forced the thought away, summoning a strained smile at Jacob's humor.

He touched her hand again. "I'm so sorry about your grandfather."

"He encouraged my love of science, helped me...be who I am."

She didn't like to cry. She'd cried the night Brian had taken the woman in front of her, but she'd done it later, alone. That night she'd been grateful for how little he visited her mind outside of work. Knowing he could hear her distress and yet hadn't come to her would have made it all even more horrible.

It hadn't really mattered, had it? No matter the tears or pain, at that point her binding to Brian was far more profound than even the marking. The human world wouldn't understand that. They'd compare her to a battered spouse, deluding herself into thinking she'd asked for the punishment. Only it had been a lesson, not a punishment, and she was part of the vampire world. As Jacob had pointed out, every servant was all too aware of why the boundaries existed.

She'd made her choice, damn it. She ignored the vicious inner voice that wanted to know where the call of destiny ended and the embrace of self-destruction began. Instead, she returned to the subject of her dying family member, safer ground. "I'm still close enough to the age when I became a servant I could go visit Grandfather, but you know the rules. We're supposed to wean ourselves off family relationships in whatever way we have to do it."

"But you haven't completely severed ties. You could still go see him."

She shook her head. "They're in Tennessee. Brian has no time in his schedule for that and he can't spare me. We're at a critical juncture on several projects."

Jacob's lips thinned as if he'd say something more, but she turned away. "Speaking of which, I better get back to this. He'll be up soon and this report needs to be ready for him."

A lie, because she was done with it. But she couldn't pursue this conversation further. She waited, tense, until Jacob stood, kissed the top of her head. "Okay, geek. You know where I am if you need anything."

"Thanks for the cookies."

"Better eat them before those rodents attack," he said as he headed for the door. "They'll be bouncing off the walls on a sugar high."

The three mice were sitting on top of the fragrant container Jacob had brought, and Emilie was already investigating the cracked lid. She slid the mice off into their cage and closed the door. "It's time for me to do some serious work," she told them. "Go play in your maze."

Three clear, colorful tubes ran out of the cage, up along the wall and across the ceiling of the lab, coming back together to one cylinder to pass through the wall to more mazes and compartments in other rooms of the research wing. She'd bought a few pieces initially to build an arch over the cage, give them a more expansive habitat, but then John, the grandson of Lyssa's majordomo, Elijah Ingram, had gotten involved. As Debra had noted, if John was involved, Lyssa's son Kane was sure to be helping as well. The boys were near constant companions during weekend nights and John's pre-bedtime hours on the weekdays, since he still attended school in town.

With a mind like a young civil engineer, John had designed the whole set up and he and Kane implemented it together, John showing the very young vampire how to help with assembly. Though Lyssa and Jacob didn't overly indulge their son, money wasn't a limitation when the project was deemed educational. Since Kane was old enough to start figuring out how things fit together, Jacob had ordered the many pieces needed. Debra had been delighted to see her three pets getting such freedom. On top of that, the boys took care of the mice when she traveled. John even handled the laborious process of cleaning out the tube sections when needed.

Just one example of the many lovely, remarkable things in her life. Her focus needed to be on that. Her Master *was* a good man, and time had made him kinder toward her. Plus, no matter what else he wasn't, in those intense sessions during feeding or lovemaking, he was everything she could want in a Master.

Service to one's vampire was what drove a servant. Though she might not feel it now, time would help her accept that, find complete fulfillment. She had the average servant's three hundred year lifespan to figure it out. It should have been a comforting thought. Unfortunately, it increased the heavy weight over her heart, so she chose the only immediate solution for it.

She got back to work.

Chapter Two

Debra, stripped naked, cowered in the shadows. She was far too pale, because they'd fed on her too long. A shadow loomed over her, a ham-sized fist wrapping in her blond hair, the usually clean and shining strands lank and oily. She was food. Nothing more, nothing less.

When she was jerked to her feet, she fought despite her weakness, because she would. Most only saw a shy, socially awkward woman with a near constant frown of concentration on her face because of the rapid-fire workings of her brain, but Brian knew her courage never faltered.

He lunged forward, but he wasn't close enough. In that cloudy shift that happened during dreams, he knew he wasn't even in the room. He was watching events unfold as if he was inside her mind but in a remote location. She was suffering all this alone. Yet he could feel her clinging to his name in her mind. She was drawing strength from her connection to him, even though he couldn't reach out to her. The loss of that connection was like death itself.

The massive vampire sank his fangs into her throat, over her windpipe, strangling her as he took the blood. He wanted to drink her dry then kill her, because he was done with her, in the mood for a new taste. He picked up a scalpel, intending to carve her heart out of her chest and dine on it, the blood alone not enough. He had to consume all of her.

No.

Brian jacked up in his bed, sheets fisted in his hands. He had a snarl on his lips, his fangs fully unsheathed. Yet he confronted a dark room where there was nothing but himself and the echo of his fury.

Damn it. Ever since the night Debra had left the facility to help Gideon and Anwyn recover Daegan Rei from rogue vampires, he'd been plagued by these dreams. Because he'd tended the handful of traumatized human women who'd been kept in cells for months by those rogues, he couldn't forget their sallow faces, hopeless eyes and trembling fear. Debra hadn't been one of them, but irrationally, he kept imposing her face on theirs in his dreams.

As yet more evidence of his illogical state, he kept having to resist the temptation to order Debra to stay with him during his sleeping hours, so she'd be close enough for him to protect. Even though he was least capable of protecting her when stuck in his daylight coma. She'd be far more likely to sacrifice herself for him in such a vulnerable state.

He was behaving like an idiot.

If he told her to stay with him during daylight hours, and if she wasn't so respectful, she'd tell him he'd lost his mind. She was as much of a workaholic as he was, and such an indulgence would cut into the time they needed to manage their ongoing projects. The workload had blossomed, so demanding she was handling half the projects herself. He checked her notes and received a daily status update, but that was to satisfy his curiosity and enjoy what strides she'd made or brainstorm about new directions, not to check her work. Though she was several decades behind him in study, she was every bit as capable a scientist as himself.

But she was his.

The feeling that thought brought had no rational basis either, but ever since that harrowing night, such primitive feelings had been surfacing more and more. Along with those dreams. It irritated him. He had no time for such things, and neither did she. Science was their focus.

Not right now, though. Dominance, sexual and otherwise, was a part of vampire nature that couldn't be denied. Discovering the depth of her submissive nature when they'd met had therefore been a pleasure, but lately he found himself fighting a growing desire to explore it even deeper, underscore it further than he'd allowed himself since the earliest days of their relationship.

It was dangerous, a desire so strong it was an obvious craving, one he had in full color right now, much like his way-too-vivid dream. He tried to push it away, tamp it down as he usually did, knowing such urges were unwise. But that animalistic side snarled at the cool rational one, sending it cowering like the Debra in his dream. And seeing that image again decided him.

Reaching out to her in his mind, he found her at her desk in the lab, a corner office she'd created to stay accessible to the staff and run tests while handling the endless emails and data review.

Debra, come to my room. Right now.

Yes, my lord. On my way.

Her mellifluous voice was a mix of everything she was. The honed syllables emphasized her intelligence, the accurate information she provided never vague or exaggerated. The breathless quality suggested experiences that would take her breath away. And then there was that tagged purr, hinting at the sensuality that he could transform to pleading desire, a treasure that put gold to shame. He thought of the moistness of her lips, the honey between her thighs, the rapid pulse in her throat, her body arching up to him. And that helpless, wide-eyed sweet disbelief she experienced, every time she surrendered to him with such need and passion.

Usually when he summoned her, he'd pull out of her mind after she responded, turn to whatever task was waiting in his private lab. He might surface a half hour later to find her sitting in a chair in his chambers, pursuing her own work until he was ready to address her. The perfect servant. He didn't do that this time, waiting impatiently, sitting on the edge of the bed, every muscle tense.

When she slipped into the room, he saw she was dressed for work as usual. Being located at the Council headquarters, she was conscious of the potential for frequent interface with higher-ranking vampires, as well as the image she needed to present to the staff. Her tailored fawn-colored skirt stopped just above the knee, and the silk shot knit shirt with a wide scoop neck bared her collar bones. Neat and clean, the outfit unwittingly complimented all her curves, her delicate neck and fine facial features.

Most servants also dressed with their vampire's blood needs in mind. Seeing the scoop collar, the vulnerability of her slim throat, her blond-brown hair pinned up on her head, made his fangs want to extend again.

They could both see in the dark, though his night vision was sharper. He saw her surprise that he hadn't turned on a lamp, wasn't already at work. But she moved toward him. "My lord? What do you need?"

As she drew closer, he inhaled her scent. He detected her mice, sunflower seeds, cookies and pencil lead. She often liked to figure organically, despite her tablet being her constant companion. She set it aside as she approached him.

That was when he detected another odor clinging to her, one that provoked an unexpected reaction he didn't resist. Catching her wrist, he had her down on her back on the bed in a blink. He drove the breath out of her as he put himself on top of her, and not just because of his solid weight. He was wearing nothing but brief shorts and an aching hard-on that insinuated itself through the thin fabric of her skirt. His gaze latched on the swell of her breasts, accentuated by her arched position and the scooped collar.

"Why was Jacob this close to you?"

Her pulse jumped in her throat, trepidation mixed with arousal. It was the type of reaction one saw in a submissive who craved a Master's touch...his discipline. He didn't offer that very often to Debra. Feeling her mind swirling between anxiety and arousal at his harsh demand, he wondered why he didn't indulge that pleasure more often. Their permutations of Dominance and submission usually focused on her compliance to his sexual desires. Not his desire to test the limits of her submission in more creative ways. Ways that were goading his bloodlust now.

"Answer me."

"I...he comes to the lab daily. He's my friend. He hugged me." Her cheeks colored as he continued to glower at her. "Servants...are very affectionate, my lord. You know this."

"Don't tell me what I know and don't know. He did more than hug you."

"He kissed the top of my head. Sat me...I sat on his lap. Just affection, my lord." Her gaze darkened. "I am yours and he belongs fully to Lady Lyssa. It's simply how servants can be."

Which you would know if you took the time to look into my mind more often.

He didn't usually, not outside of the work they did in the lab, but he did at that key moment. When he growled, she started as if he'd goaded her with a cattle prod.

"I apologize, my lord," she said, though the set of her chin made him wonder if she was truly sorry. He'd find out. "I wasn't trying to be impertinent."

"Yet you still managed it brilliantly."

Color stained her cheeks, but she said nothing further. She was obviously uncertain of this mood, but what filled his mind was she'd had that same set to her chin when she fought the enemy in his dreams. He'd let her leave that night, let her go near danger without him. Yes, he'd been needed at the Berlin castle for vital reasons related to that rescue attempt, but that wasn't the point.

He rose, bidding her with a short movement of his hand to stay in her sprawled position, legs open as much as the skirt allowed. As he studied her, her eyes lowered. But he saw how she took advantage of the demure act. Her attention lingered on his shoulders and chest, the track of his abdomen, leaving a trail of heat on his skin. Then she focused on his testicles and cock, forming a very noticeable mound under the cloth. Her aroused scent increased like that of a crushed gardenia, making him rein back a multitude of savage desires. "Stand up and take off your shoes."

As she slipped off the low, practical heels, he detected a delicious quiver to her. Had she gotten wet when Jacob touched her? The vision put murderous thoughts in his head. "Pull your panties down to your thighs. Don't take them off. Then hold your skirt up at your waist."

Her eyes widened at that. He moved to switch on the lamp, and when he turned back, she'd complied. She was wearing white lace panties. She didn't wear anything as racy as most of the servants who came through the Council headquarters did, but he'd never demanded that of her. Truth, her naked in a lab coat was enough to make him want to fuck her senseless. He'd never demanded that of her either. Maybe that was about to change.

He came back, sat down on the bed. Taking her arm, he guided her closer to him. When it became clear he was going to spank her like a child, he saw a confused tangle in her mind. He'd wanted the panties and skirt in that position because it offered an erotic humiliation. He wanted to punish her for making him fear for her life. He required her to stay safe.

All vampires had impulse control triggers. The younger the vampire, the harder it was to rein them back. He was a young vampire, yes, but not that young. His primal side might have hold of him, but he was letting it have full rein. Especially as he inhaled Jacob's scent again.

He pushed her down over his thighs. At five-eight, she was made up of willowy limbs, slender fingers and lovely feet with high arches and soft heels, her toenails painted a simple frost color like her fingernails.

When she floundered, unsure of how to brace herself in that position, he held her. "Be still," he said sharply. She went still, though he heard the erratic catch of her breath. "Part your thighs and lift your ass. I expect to feel all your muscles straining to bring it up as high as you can go. You won't lower it, no matter how much it hurts."

"No, Master."

Master. She called him *my lord* most often, but the other springing to her tongue now made triumph surge through him.

She had a pale, heart-shaped ass, one that would flush with color as easily as her cheeks did when she was flustered. He wanted to leave it red and throbbing, wanted her to ask his permission to use a pillow to sit. Would she? Or would she suffer silently? He didn't want that. He wanted her to ask him to see to her comfort.

He'd learned to suppress such thoughts, knew they were warning signs. Yet he didn't this time.

Instead, he brought his palm down on one firm cheek and she jumped, her hands curling around his bare calf. He liked the touch of her hands, so he didn't tell her to let go. He could feel the strain of her stomach muscles, and he cupped her pussy between her spread legs, probing the wetness.

"Why did you come in here already aroused? Was it Jacob?"

"No, my lord." She sounded gratifyingly shocked at the idea. "I was thinking...of when you last fed. When you had me serve you on my knees."

Now he was surprised. He enjoyed her submission intensely, but he hadn't thought of her fantasizing about it when she wasn't with him. She always seemed so focused on their work. He spanked her bottom again, with more force. She made a sound of pleasure, a plea for more. He gave her more, alternating between the cheeks and then hitting at their base, increasing the sensation as they wobbled in reaction. He began to stroke her clit as he eased his fingers into her, feeling the convulsive ripple through her cunt. She was gasping, her body quivering all the more.

"You'll serve me on your knees again when I'm done here."

"Yes, Master. Please."

He returned to spanking her, and the more he did it, the more he wanted to do it. Lifting her as easily as he could lift a vase, he set her down on the floor on her elbows and knees, ass still raised in the air as he commanded. If there was anything more stimulating than seeing his servant in that position, her arms trembling, thighs open enough he could see her flushed and glistening pussy, the small pucker of her anus, the red blush on her buttocks, he didn't know what it was. He knelt, dug his fingers into her hair, disrupting the neat coil. He massaged her scalp, his thumb passing over the occipital bone and the slender bones in the back of her neck. Then he twisted his fingers in the thick, shining strands, tight enough to pull on the scalp while still holding her head to the floor. That trembling turned into spasmodic quivers. She liked the combination of a Master's demand, the threat of pain mixed with overwhelming pleasure.

He started swatting her anew. As he started to put more force behind it, he shifted his hold to her nape, holding her in place. He knew when it started to genuinely hurt, from the choked sound of her cries, the vibrations in her mind, apprehension and desire both. She wanted him to stop but she didn't want him to stop, needing the pain because it unlocked things buried inside herself. Hurtful things.

He paused at that. She wasn't expecting it, such that she wasn't able to suppress the sound in time. A sob. It was a different sound from a pleasured gasp, more like the sharp catch that came from a sudden knife thrust inside flesh.

Yes, servants cried at times. He'd seen it happen frequently at vampire dinners, a normal reaction to unlocking the pain-pleasure connection to a submissive's emotional needs, but Debra didn't succumb to it that often.

Her buttocks were flaming red from his punishment. When he bent to kiss one cheek, nuzzling her, her fingers curled into the rug, forehead still down. She was holding back any noise now, crying silent tears, but he felt them as if they were falling inside himself.

Gripping her shoulders, he brought her up to her heels. She ducked her head, trying to hide her face from him, but he caught her chin in a firm hold, studying the tear tracks. He'd told her she'd be sucking him off after he finished spanking her. Her eyes had lowered, were already focused there. Her breathing was still erratic from her distress, but from arousal, too. He felt her anticipation. She wanted the act fiercely, wanted to immerse herself in the physical pleasure so she wouldn't feel so…empty.

He stared at her. She was his to do with as he desired. He had every right to disregard her emotions and, in truth, Debra had always dealt with them herself, suggesting she didn't need him to attend to that part of her. She was his self-sufficient, practical servant. Rational.

And she was crying.

Bending, he put his arms around her. She wasn't sure what he was about, trying to accommodate, anticipate. "Be still," he said gruffly, and she complied, uncertain and stiff as he gathered her up and took her to the bed. He didn't carry her often, but she was so light. More than most, he was aware of how fragile a human's bones were, even a third mark's—especially if it was a vampire breaking them.

That damn dream.

Laying her down, he slid into the bed with her. She was facing him, and he traced the tears on her face, her cheeks, over her lips. She looked as if she might say something, explain them away, but he shook his head, bidding her stay silent. She subsided, lashes fanning her cheeks again, a sigh lifting her shoulders. His mouth tightened. He should let it be.

Instead, he gathered her up against his chest, his thigh over hers, surrounding her. After a long, tense pause, her arms crept around his back and she let out another little sigh, going limp in his arms. Having been taken so close to subspace with that spanking, her mind was a chaotic soup, so he couldn't make heads or tails of the tears unless he wanted to delve deeper. He wasn't really used to doing that, so for now he stayed in this new territory, just holding her against him.

He stroked her hair, feeling the fine silk of it. Thinking of the dream, where it had been lank and dirty, he increased his grip.

"In the future," he said, "You may accept hugs from Jacob, the occasional pat on the shoulder, but no more sitting in his lap. Or I will make sure your ass is far too sore to sit on a chair, let alone a man's lap. Understood?"

She nodded. "Yes, Master."

Her body twitched as if he'd injected a quick jerk of arousal through her nerves. He wanted to fuck her here and now, but something held him back. He touched her mind tentatively, not wanting to hear another sarcastic remark, but what he did hear was enough to leave him pondering.

There is only one man I desire. Only one man I've ever desired like this. You.

In this position, his unsatisfied cock was against her abdomen. He could feel her concern, her sense of responsibility to tend to his needs, but as he stroked her hair, said quiet, incoherent things to her, it eased. Then she did something remarkable. She fell asleep.

Third marks had to reach an extraordinary level of stress or sleep deprivation to drop off like that. He wondered which it was. Perhaps both. Had he been pushing her too much? It frustrated him that sunlight made him too groggy to function between sunrise and dusk. Lady Lyssa called it the vampire "teenage years" because of the level of sleep vampires his age needed. Supposedly, it improved once a vampire hit his nineties, but like his impulse control, he'd hoped that part of him would mature more quickly.

Debra had taken on more and more to make up for the lost hours, keeping the projects moving forward at a brisk pace. Despite that sullen thought about him never listening to her mind, she never complained.

He thought of how it had startled her, to find he was listening. That bugged him. Thinking about a variety of things, he held her for an hour, despite the work load waiting for them. He ran his hands down her back, over the silky fabric of her shirt. He unzipped the skirt so he could slide his hand down over one bare buttock, stroke it. Her panties were still caught at her knees, and he found her sleeping in such dishabille unspeakably moving and erotic at once.

Easing her to her back, he moved the panties to her ankles. He almost removed them, but when his gaze slid up the lengths of her long, slender legs to the shadowed juncture between her thighs, barely hidden by the bunched state of the skirt, he changed his mind. He tied the panties at her ankles, holding her legs together, then slid the skirt off of her. He shed his shorts and leaned over her. Tracing the gentle swells of her breasts over the top of the shirt, he bent to lay a kiss between them. Her lashes fanned her cheeks, her pale pink lips parted, so he lifted his head to kiss them as well, tasting the soft, moist inside of her mouth with his tongue. She mumbled sleepily, her breath sweet on his face.

He had to be inside her, and he saw that desire in her mind as well, even in her somnolent haze. She loved how they lost themselves together when they were joined. That drifting thought gave him pause, but not enough to deny himself.

Shifting over her, he straddled her closed legs, then guided his cock into the narrow channel between them. He rubbed it over the petals of her sex, enjoying the pleasure of her earlier arousal coating him there. He took his time with it, at last settling down upon her, bracing his elbows on either side of her head to hold his weight, thumbs stroking her cheeks, her forehead as he pressed into her. It was an excruciatingly pleasurable position for them both, the head of his cock pushed toward the top of her channel, stroking her there in a way that would take her far longer to come, but would also make her crazy with sensation.

He knew her body so well, like no male ever had, nor ever would again. He lifted his hips to draw out slow, then pushed back in again. He stepped inside her mind, feeling her arousal grow and bring her in a pleasurable slide out of sleep, such that she was making sexy little pleas in her throat. Capturing her wrists, he stretched out her arms, holding them to the bed as he worked himself over her, his gaze delving into the depths of her brown eyes, watching her moisten her lips.

"My lord..."

"Call me the other."

"Master." Her gaze flared at that, because he'd never made that demand of her. She wanted to come, he knew she did, but something different came to her lips. "Please let me watch you come, Master. I love to see you come. Feel it happen inside of me."

"You first," he commanded quietly. "You'll come first."

Because he didn't regularly attend vampire social events or avail himself of his servant as frequently in public venues, he knew there were those who thought he wasn't as driven by his libido as a "normal" vampire, but that wasn't the case at all. When he could focus on his servant like this, he enjoyed nothing better than tormenting her to the point she was trembling like a leaf, her every moan and sigh an entreaty for release. He held her on that cusp until she was panting, gasping, wailing. His cock had thickened inside her, and he was moving even slower, feeling how her nerve endings had caught fire, her clit swollen and needy, throbbing.

"Please." She couldn't go over until he changed the angle, so he kept her on the edge, mindless, begging, calling his name. Asking to do anything for him.

"Now." He changed the thrust, and sent her catapulting. Usually she'd bite down, try not to be too loud unless he commanded otherwise, but this time he'd taken her so far on that edge she lost control and screamed out her pleasure. Desire surged in him, sending him over that same cliff, spilling his seed inside her.

The ejaculation made him feel she was even more his, like a third marking all over again. It was an emotional reaction, not a rational one. He'd learned not to give it too much credence beyond the heat of the moment, but this time as he saw her come down, the want and need in her gaze was something he couldn't resist. He lowered himself on her, pressed his mouth to her and held there. She made a questing noise against him, her palms sliding over his shoulders. He liked the way her fingers slid up into his hair, stroking. Her thighs quivered beneath the clamp of his own. Rising up, he got rid of the panties and then lay back down, guiding her legs up over his hips so he could slide back in to the hilt. She let out a keening cry, arching up to him.

"That's my servant," he murmured, kissing her jaw. He worked his way down from there, and her fingers tightened in his hair as he bit, taking a pull on that vein in her throat. He wanted her to feel the rush of lightheadedness, the reminder that her life was in his hands. Her pussy clutched him, a ripple of response, telling him the knowledge only made her want him to thrust deeper, drink harder.
I would give you anything, my lord. My life is yours.

Did she know he was in her mind? He didn't say anything, wanting to know if she would say anything further. She didn't, but he felt that sadness again.

Finished, he closed the bite mark before propping himself on one arm to look down at her. She gave him a smile, touched his mouth, running her thumb over the residual blood there. She usually kept her hands to herself until he commanded otherwise, and he always discouraged intimate little touches like that in the aftermath. Had he let this go too far? He was about to say something to take them off this too-intimate track, but she spoke first.

"I have the Helsinki figures processed," she said. "Once you're ready, my lord, we can go over them."

"All right," he said. "Go back to the lab. I'll get dressed and join you there."

He rolled off her reluctantly, watched her put her feet down on the opposite side of the bed. The curve of her back under her thin shirt was a vulnerable curve. She found her panties and skirt, slipped them back on, tucked in the shirt as well. She was talking, more information about the Helsinki data, but for once he wasn't picking up on any of that. Just watching her body language. Stiff, unsure, the language of someone holding a great deal inside.

Picking up her shoes, she nodded. "See you shortly, then."

"All right." He watched her cross the room and leave him, closing the door behind her. He listened to her pad down the hallway in her bare feet, head up the stairs. There was a pause there, as if she put on the shoes, but when he put out a questing tendril in her mind, he found she'd stopped for other reasons. She had her temple against the wall halfway up the stairs, her hand gripped tight on the railing. He felt that squeezing ache inside her, then she shoved it down, continued up the steps.

They'd gone through this in the first couple years, her adapting to the necessary reality of their relationship. He knew it had been painful for her, a difficult transition. So it was best to let it be, not re-open that can of worms. Human servants went through emotional ups and downs through the first fifty years or so of their service. All vampires knew this.

But in his extensive demographic data collection on servants, he'd discovered something less widely known. There was a greater mortality rate for full servants in those first fifty years than in any other time of their 300 year lifespan. Nearly forty percent of servants never made it past the half-century mark in a vampire's service.

A little over eighteen percent were executed by their Master or Mistress. While being fully marked was a human's choice, unfortunately the understanding of what carrying three marks meant often didn't become clear until the deed was done. Because the vampire world operated in the shadows of the human world, and secrecy was of utmost importance, a fully marked servant couldn't simply be released from service when they proved unsuitable. Such executions were done as humanely as possible, a cold comfort to the human, he was sure.

He'd at least come up with a way to deal with that, a mark remover combined with a mind eraser that was fairly effective. It was tremendously disorienting for the human, but the secret of vampire existence was protected, and the servant's life could be spared. Like most of his research, that had been driven by vampire benefit. Very few vampires relished having to execute their servant. And when a servant died, that sharp truncation of connection between vampire and servant was disorienting, emotionally and physically.

For that reason, another ten percent of new servants were lost to fights, because battles between vampires often involved taking out a servant for the same reasons warriors of old would take out a cavalry horse, hoping the momentary disorientation would help them take the head of the rider.

Then there was the last twelve percent, the group of servants whose early demise was rarely discussed.

Suicides.

He thought of Debra, the sadness in her face, and a cold feeling gripped him low in the stomach. He'd never even considered... No, she was rational. She'd never do such a thing. Like the best vampire servants, she was completely committed to his service. But finding out that it was not a reciprocal relationship emotionally was a difficult transition for most humans, used to framing a dedicated relationship in terms of marriage, family...soul mates.

Debra was the first human servant he'd chosen for himself. He was from a noble family, a born vampire whose father was a wealthy English landowner to the human world and a Region Master in the vampire world. Brian had been born to the entitlements of such privilege and was taught early the distinction between him and other vampires of lesser stock. It made the gap between vampires and humans even more of a chasm. That had been hammered home to him throughout his childhood and adolescent years. While he'd chosen a different path for vampires than his father had wanted, he was still very much a product of the culture in which he'd been raised.

Many vampires lost themselves in a servant's initial passion, forgot what the boundaries of the relationship had to be. He'd shut down any feelings like that in himself, ascribing it to a chemical urge, like endorphins. More than his family history took him down that path. Early in his studies, he'd envisioned a research facility dedicated to the vampire species. To accomplish that, he'd have to achieve credibility with much older vampires, and most doubted the maturity of a vampire prior to his first century mark. His self-control was constantly under the microscope.

Fortunately Debra had not only understood his drive in that regard; she'd matched it. She was one of the most remarkable women he'd ever met. He hoped he conveyed that in the responsibility he gave her, in the confidence he had in her findings and his overwhelming respect for her mind. But what he'd seen there tonight made him wonder if he was somehow making a grave error, overlooking something vital he needed to provide her.

He'd thought she'd reconciled herself to her role. He'd certainly taken some distastefully extreme steps to ensure it. But no matter what boundaries, protocols or lessons existed, most humans didn't understand what the relationship truly was until the first several decades had passed, and he and Debra hadn't even spent their first decade together. However, she was more mature, a faster thinker. What would take others thirty or forty years to realize, maybe she faced now.

And maybe the capricious heart alone made the decision as to what a servant could and couldn't accept. The thought disturbed him, but he pushed it away for now. Time for a shower. They had the Helsinki figures to review.

§

Brian scrolled through the latest space station data on the properties of sunlight, comparing it to data they'd culled from the ashes of vampires gathered after they chose to meet the sun. He saw some intriguing findings from Lab 6, under Debra's supervision. Nothing right now that suggested a way for vampires to endure sunlight more comfortably, but many scientific discoveries occurred as a result of seemingly unrelated leads and sifting through tons of data, just to see what random puzzle pieces turned up. One might eventually lead to the most important piece. Debra's summary statement at the end of the report reflected the same conclusion.

He was striding down the maze of hallways in the main estate compound, headed back to the research wing. As always, he was vaguely aware of servants stepping out of his path, perhaps even a couple vampires. Most of the time he didn't offend with such behavior. The visitors and occupants of the estate for the most part were accustomed to his preoccupation and didn't take it as a lack of respect. Until the day he'd forced Lady Lyssa to veer from her path to avoid a full collision with him.

He hadn't even realized she was there until he heard a startled gasp. Lifting his head, he saw Lord Uthe's servant frozen at the other end of the hall, having witnessed his transgression. He'd skidded to a halt, sensing Lyssa in the same moment. Turning, he saw her waiting on his attention—waiting, God help him—with that deadly grace she had, even in a motionless posture like she held then. She'd raised a brow.

"We're going to put a bell on you, Lord Brian. Or I'm going to start carrying a cattle prod to keep you mindful of your whereabouts."

"Yes, my lady. My deepest apologies."

Her lips quirked, the jade eyes gleaming, and then she continued up the hall without further comment. Lord Uthe's servant scurried off with a "my lord" and a hidden smile.

Since then, he'd tried to stay aware of his surroundings a little better. Which was why his head came up, his eyes narrowing when an all-too-recently-familiar scent hit him. Jacob had been out working on the grounds with the maintenance crew. He bore a sheen of sweat on bare skin, since he was stripped to his jeans, a T-shirt tossed carelessly over his shoulder. His lean, powerful body was as much a warrior's as a servant's. The virile display pricked that knot of ugly feelings Brian thought had dissipated.

When Jacob saw Brian, he offered a courteous nod. "Lord Brian."

He should have offered his usual distracted acknowledgement, but as Jacob passed him, Brian stopped. Not just because of his own feelings on things. The cut of Jacob's glance wasn't his usual pleasant manner, either.

"Jacob."

The servant came to a halt and turned, raised a brow. "My lord."

No mistaking the coldness that time. Brian set his tablet on a side table and stepped toward him. Interestingly, Jacob closed the distance. Even realizing his objectivity was not at its best level today, Brian found himself matching that aggressive stance toe to toe.

Jacob was an intelligent, loyal servant and an exceptional male, one whose courage, service and dedication to his lady had impressed Brian on numerous occasions. But right now he didn't care about that. He was remembering that scent on Debra's skin, the flush when he confronted her about it. She liked it when this male hugged her, paid attention to her.

"Is there a problem?" Brian ground out, aware that the tips of his fangs were showing. Jacob's gaze flickered over them, but it didn't modulate his attitude at all.

"Not with me, my lord. But perhaps if you add Debra to your task list on that little device of yours, you could manage a thought toward her wellbeing. Since she sacrifices all of herself to yours."

"Isn't that a servant's job?"

Jacob's lip curled. "Pompous asshole isn't a good look for you, Brian."

He wasn't one to act on physical impulses. Yet a blink later he had Jacob shoved up against the wall, so forcefully he heard the male's bones thud against the brick. Despite that, Jacob didn't submit. Instead, he swung up between Brian's arms and struck his chin with both fists, hard enough the vampire saw stars. Though Brian had him multiple times over on strength, Jacob was called to fight far more often than a research scientist. Brian tasted blood from his split lip and saw red. He was going to rip his fucking arms off.

He pulled Jacob off the wall, flung him toward the floor. Jacob rolled and was on his feet in an instant, squared off with him. The idiot servant wasn't backing down, his expression hard.

"You tread on dangerous ground, Jacob."

"I'm a vampire's servant, my lord. That goes without saying." Jacob cracked his neck, rotated his shoulders. "Want to try again? I'm sure I can get in a couple more punches. It'd be worth some broken bones to me."

Brian blinked. "It's an executable offense to attack a vampire."

"Only if I'm trying to kill you. I've no intention of that."

"No chance of that," Brian retorted.

Jacob grinned. It reminded Brian that more than once this man had been a vital ally, someone willing to protect Lyssa with his life and very soul if needed. Damn it, he liked the man. Biting back his irritation, he struggled to get his inexplicable caveman reaction under control.

"I know your lady's regard for you, Jacob, and I acknowledge your value as well, but on occasion you forget your place."

"Not on occasion." Jacob snorted. "Pretty much constantly, if you ask her."

"You will keep your hands off Debra except in the context of your Mistress's command," Brian snapped.

It startled Jacob as much as it had shocked Debra, Brian could tell. But Jacob rallied quickly, his brow creasing with concern, protective instincts kicking in. "If you think she's done anything inappropriate or disloyal to you, my lord, you really do have your head up your ass."

"I don't think that," Brian ground out. "Are you trying to get me to put your head through the wall?"

"She loves you with everything she is," Jacob said, blue eyes intent. "If that doesn't demand reciprocity in your version of the vampire-servant relationship, it at least deserves acknowledgement. Respect. Appreciation."

"She's brilliant. I tell her that often."

Jacob closed his eyes, astonishingly as if he was seeking patience with a particularly thick-headed child. Brian really was going to rip off his limbs. He'd figure out an explanation for Lyssa. Which would probably gain him an extra ten seconds before she separated him from *his* appendages.

Jacob opened his eyes, met Brian's gaze. "We give up everything for you. Willingly, because of what we receive in return. I know you think highly of her mind. Maybe you should pay closer attention to what's going through it. And her heart. If that doesn't matter to you, you haven't grown up as much as I thought you had, these past few years."

"I'm getting tired of insults."

"I'm not insulting you." Jacob sighed, ran a hand over his face. "You spoke to Council, explained why you think some vampires are more disposed to childbearing."

Brian nodded stiffly. "Yes."

"Then practice what you preach." Jacob's eyes sharpened and he stepped forward so he was once again close to Brian, but it was a different kind of confrontation now. "The bond I have with my lady? It's the very air I breathe, my lord. Knowing she has given me her heart, that she entrusts me with her love, it's indescribable. We can all talk about unconditional service until we're blue in the face, but reciprocity is what strengthens a relationship, makes it something we can't live without."

His visage darkened. "When a soul like Debra's has to live without it, it's a half-life. A very painful one. Yes, servants understand the nature of our relationship with vampires, but we also understand deeper things about that relationship that sometimes you all miss. When you deny us any part of your souls, you might as well tear our hearts out of our chests, because carrying them around becomes eternal torment."

Stepping back, he gave Lord Brian a short bow, then pivoted and headed down the hallway. "Don't tie up your hands in combat," he threw over his shoulder. "I could have staked you while you were trying to choke me."

Brian bared his fangs at that, but Jacob was already headed up the long corridor. He should ask Lyssa to have him publicly whipped. She might get some pleasure out of that, if done right. But he wouldn't ask, because Jacob was right. Brian didn't believe in pompous displays of vampire power over human servants.

The male should at least wear a shirt in the hallways, though.

Watching a pair of female staff staring after Lyssa's servant, seeing their obvious appreciation for the glistening broad shoulders and how denim cupped his ass, annoyed Brian greatly. It was distracting and...indecent.

When they turned and saw him, both servants gave a respectful bow and headed off to their duties. It only irritated him more.

Chapter Three

His lack of control was intolerable. He knew Debra's mind, her devotion to him. If she accepted the platonic affection of a friend, it was nothing that interfered with her loyalty to him.

He and Debra worked well into the early evening hours with the other members of the research staff. They handled conference calls, sample processing, countless emails and write ups. He pushed all of them, wanting to immerse himself in the things he understood.

When he was finally forced to retire with the dawn, he knew there were about three more hours of samples to analyze. She assured him she and the staff would handle it. He studied her face, touched her mind, felt nothing but sincerity. Vaguely dissatisfied, he gave her a short nod and headed for his quarters below ground.

Once there, though, he found he couldn't sleep. He could push away his irrational reaction to Jacob. Pushing away his words wasn't as easy.

He had some time before the sunrise above ground would force him to sleep. He owed his father an email, but he didn't have the concentration for it. His quarters were well-appointed, with a small lab and office area, sitting room, comfortable bed, paintings and artifacts collected on his travels. Passing his fingers over a wood carving of a slender woman, a pleasing thing given to him by an overlord in Tunisia, he realized he didn't feel like doing any of the normal things he did to unwind, prepare for sleep. Perhaps he should have recommended the research facility be located in Alaska, where night held far greater dominion over the hours.

With a sigh, he stripped and lay down on the bed, cut the lights. Not entirely sure of his purpose, he nevertheless decided to enter Debra's mind and silently observe. Record, collect data, the way he might for an experiment. A very important one, where every detail was vital to reaching the proper conclusion.

She was still working. Since she was alone, he assumed the lab techs were busy in other wings, processing blood samples with electrophoresis and examining DNA segments with PCR. She was bent over her microscope, patiently examining slide after slide and making notes. She was so thorough, never rushing any process. But she did pause to rub her eyes, Picking up the bottle next to her, he saw it was a caffeine energy drink, something third marks didn't normally need. Carefully screwing the top back on after taking a draught, she rolled her head back on her shoulders. He could feel the knots in her muscles, the tension in her lower back.

When he heard Jacob's voice, he stiffened. However, as the male entered the lab, laid a hand on her shoulder, Brian could feel her response at every level. It truly was a strong friendship, one that brought her comfort and made Brian feel petty for resenting it. Jacob massaged her shoulder with that one hand, picking up on her discomfort. He could see the male servant's concern. So he wasn't the only one noticing how hard she was pushing herself. Though Jacob had been noticing far longer, perhaps explaining why he stopped by so frequently. And why he'd spoken to Brian the way he had.

When was the last time Brian had asked Debra how her day had gone? Of course, it wasn't required that he do so.

Pompous asshole.

It wasn't Jacob's voice in his head that time, but his own. He'd taken the path never traveled by a vampire, into science and research. While his father had been disappointed that Brian's interests had lain in promoting the wellbeing of the race as a whole, which meant rubbing elbows with the least as well as the highest ranking of their kind, the credit he'd been given by Council in the past few years, including this research facility, had helped his father reconcile himself to his son's choice.

Not that that was much of an issue to Brian. He loved and respected his father, but his path had always been clear. He'd sought knowledge and scientific pursuit almost as soon as he was aware of his capacity to think.

So if he'd been that much of a maverick, why was he letting the protocols of a lifetime dictate to him, when it was clear things were changing for vampire-servant relationships?

If he viewed his servant as most vampires did, with fondness and appreciation for their value, but no untoward romantic feelings, it wouldn't be an issue. But he'd liked her from their first meeting. Had wanted her intensely only a blink later. So ever since the full marking, he'd dedicated himself to shutting down both their responses, making sure everything between them was within the appropriate boundaries.

He'd done the job all too well. Or had he? Did the same feelings seethe inside Debra that seemed to be struggling to break free inside him?

She was so formal with him. It hadn't always been that way. When they first met at the lab where she worked, before she'd known he was a vampire and even for a while afterwards, she'd laughed around him, blushed, tried flirting with him a little. Spoken her mind. She was well informed on almost everything, his Debra.

With the workload they now carried, there wasn't much time to socialize, but that didn't explain it. He thought of the bond shared by pairings like Lyssa and Jacob. As busy as Lyssa was with Council matters, Brian had no doubt she checked on Jacob's mental state throughout the day, doing what he was doing now, drifting in and out of his servant's mind to get an honest picture of how she was feeling, how much she was demanding of herself. Servants were notorious for always putting their vampires first, minimizing their own needs. It was part of being a servant and certainly added to their value, but there was a line. Jacob had implied...

No, not implied. He'd stated outright that Brian completely ignored that line.

It mattered to Brian that she was tired, that her back hurt. Yes, Debra was a competent, intelligent woman capable of taking care of herself. She was also a highly-driven, obsessive compulsive submissive to whom serving her Master, never failing his expectations, was paramount. Only since he wasn't telling her what those expectations were, she was setting them, and putting that bar up on the moon.

As Jacob took his leave and Brian continued to hover in her mind, he was reminded how enchanting it was to watch Debra work. While she studied slides containing thin-sliced tissue preps, she typed in data one-handed and carried on a running commentary with her mice about that data, peppered with affectionate comments about their behavior. As always when doing tissue work, the mice were in their cage and maze tubes, but he noticed they liked to stay near, listen to her voice. He found it pleasing as well.

All those years ago, after he'd given her the first mark, he'd taken a step prohibited by Council. He'd not only let her know what he was, he'd given her a detailed account of what a fully marked servant could expect in his world. The Council overlooked—reluctantly—letting a first mark go only if that person had the vaguest knowledge or none at all of the vampire world. But he'd trusted her. Her intellect was a match for his own, such that he felt like they already stood inside one another's minds. He wasn't going to pull her all the way into his world when she wasn't ready for what that meant.

Though he'd told her all the opportunities that awaited her as a scientist, he'd also drawn a highly accurate, graphic picture of the demands placed on a vampire's servant, as well as their lack of status in his society. When he was done, she'd been pale, her eyes wide, a slight tremor in her hands. He'd wanted to reassure her, but he'd forced himself to stay silent, wait for any questions she had.

"So I'd be yours, entirely." Her brown eyes fixed on his face.

Something primitive stirred in him at the way she said it. His attention locked on her soft lips, how she swallowed under his steady gaze.

"Entirely. No rights but what I give you." He fought back the overwhelming desire to sugarcoat it. He wanted this woman as his servant the way he craved blood. That alone was a warning to let her go. It made him sharpen his tone. "But I'm not the highest ranked in my world. There are others who will have the right to make demands of you and I…have to capitulate to them."

He cleared his throat at her unreadable look. "Tomorrow night will be my last day here. If you decide to come with me, I'll need your timetable for resigning and joining me at our facility in Alabama. If you don't choose to come with me…"

He hadn't been able to stop himself from reaching out, touching her face, the slim jaw, but then he drew his hand back, forced his tone to be as flat as if he were conducting a job interview. "If you don't come with me, it's been a pleasure working with you."

When he'd retired at dawn and replayed it all in his mind, he was sure she would decline. They'd only spent a few days together, after all.

Yet though her submissive nature and cravings were a bottomless pool he'd only begun to explore, he'd intuitively recognized them as a mesh with the extreme demands of the vampire world and the type of servants who inhabited it. But she was socially awkward to the point of charming shyness. On top of that, she was an accomplished scientist and a woman well integrated into a modern Western society.

How could she possibly agree to such an offer? *"Come with me—you'll have a fabulous lab, but you'll also be a sex slave with no protection but what I can provide."* It was ludicrous for him to expect her to agree to that.

She'd shown up at the lab on time the next evening, a little more quiet and hollow-eyed, telling him she hadn't slept. She hadn't addressed the question immediately, and he'd held his tongue, not wanting to push. He expected he was putting off her rejection as long as possible. They'd worked through the early hours with minimal conversation, but as the night progressed and they started trading data, looking over one another's shoulders and brainstorming what they were analyzing, their intuitive understanding of one another's thought processes overcame the awkwardness of things unsaid.

"If you were a second mark, we'd be in each other's heads. Think how much faster we could do the calculations and theorizing. And having a third mark...it's like sharing one mind."

He'd said it without thinking, fully caught up. He remembered how serious she'd gotten then. She'd paused a long moment. Then nodded to herself, as if she'd come to some type of irrefutable conclusion. Crossing the lab to where he sat on a stool, she moved between his spread knees. Her liquid brown eyes, framed by a fringe of lashes so black they made her look like she wore eyeliner, enhancing her pale, smooth face, had fixed onto his. Pulling her ponytail over her shoulder, she averted her chin in a delicate move, offering him her throat.

He was always a man who kept his passions under tight control. Yet when she offered her neck, he struck like a cobra, banding an arm around her waist and yanking her to him. She'd gasped, but her fingers had dug into his arms, holding fast. He'd felt her nipples peak against him, the insistence of her body revealing her response to his strength. He hadn't even thought to use the pheromone mix that could ease the burn of the second mark serum, for the pain just seemed to goad her pleasure. He surged off the stool, carrying her to the nearest wall with her legs wrapped around his hips.

He'd gotten the necessary clothes out of the way and thrust into her with his fangs still in her throat. No finesse, just sheer brute demand. She was as slick as if he'd had his mouth between her legs. Feeling the clamp of her cunt on his cock, the quiver of her spread thighs against his pelvis, he didn't ever want to stop.

"Third mark," she whispered in his ear. "Please. Do it."

Struggling for some rationality, he seized her hair, pulled her head back to stare into her eyes. "Do you understand what it all means?"

"It doesn't matter," she said. And then the second mark kicked in and he heard the first words directly from her mind. *There's nothing I will ever want as much as you.*

Christ.

Tuning back in to the present, Brian saw her step outside, taking a break in the little courtyard garden outside her lab. Lifting her head to the sun, she noticed how pretty the day was, blue skies and fluffy clouds, a bright sun. Another perk to having a servant was the ability to see the sun, enjoy it through her. She registered the heat on her skin as she inhaled the flowers in the garden. She thought about sitting down on one of the benches, taking a quick cat nap.

As she sank down on the bench, she took a breath. Then another. The hints of sadness he'd sensed suffused her like a flood. It almost drove him from her mind, an instinctive retreat from the unexpected crash of emotion.

Bowing her head, she began to weep.

What the hell? Earlier, he hadn't taken the time to penetrate the chaos in her mind to see the source of her distress, but now he was neck deep and refused to let himself turn away from it. He took those tentative steps into an area he hadn't allowed himself to go before. A moment later, he floundered in a labyrinth of emotions, the depth of which startled him.

In this sad, dark place in her subconscious, Debra apparently kept everything she felt wasn't appropriate to share with anyone else. Including him. He had an intuitive sense that this maze of tunnels and perilous chasms had been a manageable space at one time. But she'd kept carving further into herself, trying to bury it lower and lower, until she was tunneling through her core.

It was like ants weakening the root system of a tree. He felt her despair. Life wasn't worth living anymore, not if it was always going to be like this.

He had to bite back a startled response to that, a demand that she talk to him, explain this, not ever consider such a thing as…leaving him. As he brought himself under control, he wondered if she sensed him. She'd wrapped her arms around herself and was rocking, softly whispering his name, a chant of comfort.

Whenever he confronted a seemingly incomprehensible tangle of data, he would start from the outer edges and work his way inward. So he forced himself past her pain to find the entry point of her distress.

Her grandfather. He was ill, dying. As soon as Brian targeted that thought, he was overrun with images of the man. With Debra as a child, a teenager, at her graduation, whenever she accepted awards, when she earned her master's degree. Early on in their time together, Brian remembered her talking about the man, a prominent figure in any personal references about her life and family.

The mortality of a servant's family was a transition all servants endured. However, feeling it as she felt it made him feel far less detached from it. But beyond that, what startled him was what surrounded all of it.

Debra was profoundly lonely.

That first night he spent in the lab with her, Debra had remained with him until dawn, even though he knew she was scheduled to work that day. When he'd protested, she'd said she wanted to make sure he didn't have any difficulties using the lab instruments. She'd also wanted the opportunity to learn as much as she could from him during his temporary visit. In between waiting on sample results, they'd talked of countless things. The colleague who had given him use of the lab had told him Debra was shy, would likely say less than ten words to him while he was there.

But the damn woman knows everything, Brian. I expect she'll be running the place in five years.

He wasn't disposed to being chatty while working himself, yet he couldn't seem to stop talking to her. During the daylight hours, he missed her, even in sleep. He regretted not being able to tell her everything she wanted to learn. For the first time since his maturity, he considered taking a full servant.

She wasn't close to the servants in the lab or on the estate. Jacob was probably her only true friend, though most the others treated her with kindness and respect. Like Brian himself, she tended to be in her head so much it was difficult for her to focus on the minutiae of small talk. The things that interested her the most she assumed no one else would want to talk about.

A smile touched his lips as he recalled her telling him how she'd dissected a variety of creatures through her childhood. Their lives had been claimed by circumstance—road kill for the animals, natural lifespan for the insects. Even so, she'd relayed her mother's horror, the first time she'd discovered her daughter investigating a rabbit's intestines in their basement.

She was on the phone with a psychologist the next day, trying to figure out if I was a budding serial killer.

But he couldn't rationalize that it was a lack of friends making her so lonely now. He was sitting in the midst of that labyrinth, and all tunnels came back to him. Her Master. He'd thought that she fed herself adequately on what science and sex could offer, but her heart was as hungry as his would be without blood for a month.

I don't need him to be like a human boyfriend. I just need to feel…that he's my Master. That I'm… She was talking to herself in that way a person did when crying, all the thoughts tangled in a rush of feeling, but even then she couldn't voice it. As the emotions battered him like waves breaking against his own heart, he filled in the words she didn't.

That she's important to me. Now he understood why Jacob had acted like he was a clueless idiot when he spouted off about how brilliant Debra was. She knew that. She needed something different from him. So very different.

Two years into their relationship, Debra had told him she loved him, and asked if he felt the same about her. It was as if she'd forgotten everything he'd told her back when she had the first mark. That had been his fault, because he'd allowed their relationship to get so familiar, so comfortable, so…close. The next night, he'd taken a female vampire in front of her, Lady Carmela. He knew he needed to teach his servant a never-to-be-forgotten lesson about the vampire-servant relationship.

Though it had sat in his gut like food poisoning for weeks afterward, he hadn't questioned his action. He'd told himself it protected her and him. He'd been relieved when she pulled out of the pain, finding a quiet dignity and strength to continue to serve him as she always had. Truth, that had surprised and impressed the hell out of him, but he'd forced himself to conceal that reaction. He'd made himself pull back, become far more reserved with her.

Yet was it possible he'd done such a harsh and cruel thing because her admission of love had spooked him? Because his own feelings for her had developed so strong and fast, he was afraid of losing everything he was working for? As a result, had he driven the lesson home like a railroad stake, when a pin prick would have been sufficient?

On certain issues, a scientist had to factor bias into his calculations. He'd worked so hard at appearing mature and in control, perhaps he'd made a horrible misstep by ignoring the fact he *was* immature in some ways. Particularly about relationships. And Debra had paid the price.

Vampires didn't have relationships, he told himself. They had bonds forged from power hierarchies. Yet servants were their closest intimate bond, impossible to describe to anyone who hadn't experienced it. Perhaps vampires avoided the irony of that by fanatically insisting it was a functional, master-slave relationship, and not what it truly was: Their only chance to establish a soul-deep trust with another being, meet that craving for love and connection that the human species accepted as a worthy goal. But unlike vampires, the human species—for the most part—had learned how to sit down at dinner without killing one another.

Our structure, our rules, are the only things that keep us from one another's throats, Brian. His father's voice, a lecture he'd heard over and over. I was part of the Territory Wars. You don't understand what we become without structure. These rules have a purpose.

The dawn lassitude was pulling him down, making it hard to think. He fought it. He couldn't leave her feeling like this. Damn it...

Debra.

She lifted her head, wiping away her tears. *My lord?*

I want you to come sleep with me. When you get here, I may already be asleep, but you will stay with me until I wake. Lie down with me and sleep as well.

But I have to finish the—

It will wait. Your Master gave you an order, Debra.

She froze at that. The sensual threat went through her like an ocean cavitation. In a drowsy haze, he watched her wrap up what she was doing, but only the minimum necessary so the results weren't ruined. Then she locked up the lab and was moving through the corridors. Coming to him.

Debra.

Yes...Master?

He smiled. *Take off your clothes before you come to bed with me. I expect my servant to be available to me in all ways when I wake.*

He stayed conscious long enough to feel the ripple of reaction through her again, know that he'd elevated her pulse and made her heart beat faster. Then the dawn reached out to claim him.

§

She wasn't sure what was going on, but his tone of voice, the purring promise of it, scattered her concentration. If he *had* wanted her to finish what she was doing before coming to him, she was pretty sure she wouldn't have trusted her results.

His chambers on the underground level of the estate always smelled of the cool earth that surrounded it, a soothing scent. She paused at his door, unsure if he'd changed his mind. But as he'd said, he was likely asleep by now. His words had been slurred when he spoke in her mind. She wouldn't second guess him.

Slipping in the room, she saw she was right. He was motionless on the bed, a tempting silhouette. Though his inability to stay awake past a certain time frustrated him, it gave her an opportunity to observe him now. He rarely invited her into his bedchamber after he was fully asleep.

First she obeyed his orders, taking off all her clothes and folding them neatly on the dresser. He had a mirror in here, which he used for looking at objects from different directions, since he didn't show up in the reflection. She caught a glimpse of herself in it, a pale, owl-eyed ghost floating across the room.

He had towers of files on most of the flat surfaces. His smaller lab, sitting room and spacious bathroom was through another door, but he tended to stack things in there as well. Every once in a while she helped him scan and load hard copies onto his computers, keeping the data in an organized fashion. But Brian had far more diverse interests than just the active projects.

Stacked up against the legs of one table were old science journals and sci-fi novels he collected from a variety of places, his form of leisure reading. On the book shelves, in front of his extensive library, he kept artifacts from his travels. She touched the statue of a slender woman that always reminded her of a willow tree. She thought the artist had intended it that way.

There were also randomly collected things, like rocks, shells, fossils. He was endlessly curious about everything, and she wondered what he'd found interesting about those particular pieces. They'd stopped talking about anything much beyond their work. It was easier that way, wasn't it? Apparently for him, too.

Biting back the pain at that thought, she left off her examination of his belongings. Brian preferred a queen-sized bed, versus the oversized king most other vampires liked in their guestrooms when visiting the estate. He said he had no desire to sleep on a padded racket ball court. She smiled at that, then slid into the bed. Feeling absurdly brave because he was asleep, and because he'd asked her to do something as intimate as sleep with him, she tugged the light sheet down.

He wasn't wearing anything. Usually he wore those brief shorts, a clingy garment that hugged him high on the thighs and elsewhere in very appealing ways. He often made jokes about his looks. How, if not for vampire metabolism, he'd be a typical soft-bellied, sallow lab goblin, but she had her doubts about that. All vampires trained to protect themselves, which included ensuring their stamina was enhanced even beyond what the gods had blessed them with. Brian did strength training with weights as well as punishing ten mile runs along the paths of the vast estate and marshlands. During those workouts, he listened to audio books and articles he downloaded to multitask, but the end result was that the muscles she saw now weren't all supernatural-made.

Plus, the man was always active, never still. It was nothing to him to climb up a sheer cliff face to examine the type of nest that might be on the top ledge, or walk to the bottom of a river bed to get a silt sample. Unlike most vampires who disliked the water because of their lack of buoyancy, he found such weighted density—and no need for scuba gear—useful for underwater data collection.

She folded her hands beneath her cheek on the pillow and gazed at him. He had an aristocratic bearing, six feet with a good breadth of shoulders, tapered waist and fine buttocks and thighs. Freeing one of her hands, she slid her fingers over those areas, barely touching him, but then it was too much to resist. With the mood she'd been experiencing these past few days, she needed to touch him. Perhaps the intimacy would ease her heart, fill the emptiness in her soul.

When awake, his intellect gave his mouth and brow creases that emphasized his intimidating intellect and emotional maturity. But asleep, those lines smoothed. He would always look like a young thirty-something, as most born vampires did once they passed that age, but he had fine features. Pretty, some would say, especially combined with his sandy-colored hair and punch-right-to-a-woman's-heart hazel eyes. She thought of the times she'd seen them rest on her with total absorption. It happened during sex, sometimes during feeding, or when their minds did that tangled DNA thing, coming to the same conclusion as if they were one soul. She cherished each of those moments, even though they were as addictive as a drug, leaving her wanting more.

When she had time, she collected data on other pending projects. One of those was servant suicide data. While she was smart enough to know not to dwell on that subject when her mood was already low, she couldn't help but think of a journal entry one servant had left. When his Mistress had given Debra the stack of diaries, Debra had asked her if she'd read them. The woman had looked at her as if she'd accused her of reading children's books for leisure, and shook her head. But Debra noticed her hand lingered on the top journal as if the vampire could still feel his life force there, and maybe she could.

I know what they say the relationship is supposed to be, but if that's the case, why does it feel this way? When I first felt my Mistress's touch upon my soul, I thought I'd never know what it was to be lonely again. Now I realize that to be given that feeling and then have it taken away, nothing more than a temporary feeling from their side of things, is far, far worse. You never get over having that and then not having it again. It leaves you feeling terminally lonely.

She trailed her fingers down the valley of Brian's spine, to his lower back, the upper rise of his buttock. He was sleeping on his stomach, arms wrapped around the pillow. It made her reach for the curve of his biceps with the other hand, following that impressive rise. She was a woman who was attracted to a man's mind first, not his body, but her Master had quite a body.

With a smile, she admitted he was probably right about what kind of body he'd have as a mortal, if he wasn't as physically active as he was now. He had the eating habits of a teenager, a considerable sweet tooth and a craving for junk food. Though she'd seen him sit down to samplings of gourmet fare prepared by incredible chefs, typically he picked politely at such offerings. One night after such a dinner she'd come back to the lab to find him with a snack bag of Cheetos. He was savoring the two or three his vampire digestive track could absorb, and then he offered the rest to Maggie, one of Lyssa's Irish wolfhounds. The elderly dog didn't run with the pack so much anymore, instead reaping the benefits of tagging after a vampire carrying around too much food.

He'd even dropped one of the Cheetos into the top of her mice's cage, to her amusement. He had opposed her having the mice, but hadn't forbidden them as long as they didn't cause hygiene issues in the research areas. Since then, she thought he'd actually gotten fond of them. One day she'd seen him looking up. He'd discovered them assembled just over his head, watching what he was doing as seriously as interns. He'd smiled, reached up with a pointer to tap the plastic tube, then went back to what he was doing.

She curved her fingers over his shoulder, slid over the biceps again. Where his other hand was wrapped around the pillow, she outlined his fingers, then rested the tops of hers on his. He kept his nails short and impeccably clean.

Curling her hand into a loose ball, she ran her knuckles down his side, over his rib cage, the layers of firm flesh. He was beautiful, and it made her heart hurt to look at him. She was so tired.

I love you, Master. I'm sorry. This would be so much easier if I didn't feel that way, if I could figure out how to love you without wanting...more. If I could figure out the chemical composition of want and desire and remove it, I would. I just don't know if I can do this for three hundred years. I always thought I could be a selfless, unconditional love kind of person, but I'm falling short in that area.

With a sigh, she curled up next to him, pillowing her cheek in the small of his back, her head cradled in that dip between chest and backside. She furrowed her hand up between the pillow and the clasp he had on it. When he instinctively changed his grip to her hand, she closed her eyes. Sweet heaven. Just to lie here and hear his heartbeat, feel his heat against her, hold his hand and imagine he was consciously holding it back.

She wished she'd never wake. That she could fall asleep like this, and let it be the last feeling she carried with her into eternity.

As she drifted off, her breathing evening out, Brian slid his hand more securely around hers, held on. *You don't go to eternity without me, Debra.* But she was already gone, and he couldn't hold out another second. It had taken all the energy he had to be still under her touch, listen to the poignant meandering of her mind.

He followed her into sleep.

§

And came out of it with a sharp jerk and snarl. Thrashing, he flung himself out of bed, and only vampire reflexes landed him on his feet.

"My lord. Brian."

He shook off the haze of sleep and nightmare, spinning on the ball of his foot to see her sitting up in the center of the bed, her hair disheveled, eyes wide in her elfin face. She had such fragile features. Another thing that made people underestimate her strength. He saw she looked better rested, and a glance at the clock said it was a couple hours past sundown. They'd both overslept.

"The Council update." She realized it at exactly the same time he thought it in his mind, and she was out of the bed in a flash. She'd folded her short lab coat over the chair by the neat pile of her clothes and grabbed it now, shrugging it on against the early evening chill even as she hurried to pull clothes out of his closet for him. Because she used her third mark speed, she had them delivered to his side a second before she flashed into the bathroom, heating the sink water so he could do a quick face wash and hair brushing.

Watching her fly around in just the lab coat and nothing else reminded him of his earlier fantasy. His cock, already in full fledge "morning" mode, which was the same for vampire or human males, only at different waking times, got even harder. When she hurried by him this time, he proved he was faster, catching her around the waist and putting her up against the wall.

"My lord," she gasped, her slim fingers landing on his shoulders. "You have to be in Council chambers in ten minutes."

"This won't take long." He wrapped her hair in his fist, and put his mouth on hers, so fiercely his fangs scraped her. She made a sexy little mewl, her hips tilting to him, her arms banding around his shoulders, and then he probed her with the head of his cock. She reached down between them, stroking the fluid already gathering on her labia walls to the outer petals to lubricate his path. He slid into her, and she made a hum at his thick waking size, which had been significantly augmented by watching her run around in the coat, the tails flapping enough to show him the lower curves of her sweet ass, her breasts quivering in the shadows of the fabric tempting further exploration.

Ten minutes, she'd said. He didn't care about coming. He just wanted to plow into her, mark her, stretch her. She held on, her moans torn between pleasure and discomfort. He held her between the point of possession and completion and kept himself there as well.

When she was writhing on him, hot and needy, and he was close to going himself, he stopped. "Look at me, Debra."

She obeyed, her gaze glazed and wet lips parted. Seeing her here, alive, unharmed, made that damnable nightmare step back, though it didn't lessen his need. "Hold onto me, tight as you can."

She slid her arms around his shoulders, her legs crossing over his hips as he helped with that, hitching her close. He banded his own arms around her, a full embrace, heart to heart, body to body. Vampires didn't need to breathe, but he wondered if he could have managed it regardless. She was here, she was all right.

"Master…" Her whisper against his ear was laden with questions as much as arousal.

Holding them both against the wall, he began to rock against her, using that finite range of space to thrust, rub against her clit.

"Come for me, Debra. Or I'll be late to Council meeting and it will be your fault."

She gave a half sob, half snort at that, and it made him grin as well, despite their intensity. He reached between them to stroke and pinch and she came apart. As the climax squeezed down on him and she cried out against his ear, breath hot against his flesh, he came as well, thrusting hard to completion as she kept moaning her pleasure, holding onto him as if she'd never let him go. Her nails cut into his flesh during her aftershocks, and he relished those bites of pain.

He wanted to come down slow, drift back over to the bed, hold her in the curve of his body for another hour or so. But she was right. Now they were down to five minutes. He let her down with an extra squeeze, a swat on her delectable ass. "Get dressed. I can't go before Council without your detailed brain with me. God only knows what I'd mess up."

She gave him a look that he could only define as…happy. It was fleeting, but his own response bemused him. His heart swelled, ridiculously. It had been a long time since she'd looked like that, and he was glad to be the cause of it. Even as the knowledge that he was likely the cause of her not looking that way far more often gave him an entirely different set of things to think about.

Three minutes later they were headed down the hallway at a fast clip, Debra typing away on her tablet to call up the information they'd need for the short update. Then she caught the sleeve of his coat, tugging him to a halt. Putting the tablet under her arm and her stylus in her teeth, she straightened his tie, smoothed down his sweater vest. The pocket protector he kept in his shirt pocket made the left side lumpy, especially stuffed with pens and his handheld. He'd typically reach down the vee neck of the vest to retrieve anything he needed, but he saw her lips twitch as they often did when she touched that spot.

"You told me when we met that I dress like a nerd," he said, curling a loose strand of her long blonde hair behind her ear. She'd caught the bulk of it back in a barrette, but she'd missed a piece.

Her cheeks turned pink. "You do, my lord. Or a college professor. I like how you dress."

"Because it gives you the opportunity to make fun of me. I liked how you were dressed this morning." He caressed her chin. "It gives me the chance to tease you a different way. Think I'll have you dress that way again. Maybe for a future Council update. Then they won't care if I get every blasted number wrong."

She blushed even more prettily then. He'd forgotten how she showed everything on her face. Christ, had he really had his head that much up his ass, like Jacob said?

It wasn't a full Council meet, thank God. That would have interfered with the whole day's schedule. This was just Lyssa, Lord Mason and Lord Uthe who, as her right hands, were visiting on other matters and had requested a quick update on their active projects. It didn't mean he could treat it with any less respect than a full Council meet, though. When they arrived, he was surprised to see another attendee he hadn't expected. But then, this male didn't usually announce his schedule. Beyond the Council members, most vampires who knew his identity didn't live very long to tell anyone about it.

Daegan Rei was the Council's assassin, charged with hunting and executing vampires who'd broken the vampire code to the point it endangered the species as a whole. Unfortunately, due to some unwise policy decisions from previous Councils, he'd been busy these past couple years, mostly dealing with the sires of made vampires who'd been turned without Council permission. Then there were the made vampires themselves, many too unstable to be allowed to survive.

Daegan was a dark-eyed, intense lean shadow of a vampire. Though he wasn't as old as Lady Lyssa, their ages weren't far apart. If ever Council made an enemy of him, he'd be a formidable one to overcome. It might take both Lyssa and Mason—the third oldest vampire— to take him down.

Fortunately, Daegan Rei was a strong supporter of Lady Lyssa. Plus, they were bound by familial relations, of a sort. Glancing left, Brian saw Gideon, Daegan's servant as well as Jacob's brother, leaning against the far wall, since servants weren't typically invited to sit during formal vampire occasions. Though Gideon was full servant to two vampires, Anwyn wasn't in the chamber. As a fledgling, she wasn't part of Council sessions, even those where the servants of Council vampires were. Brian expected she knew all that went on in them regardless, since she was fully capable of scouring Gideon's mind. Excluding her was more of a procedural issue.

He made a mental note to see how her seizure management was going while she was here. Though he didn't have his mind open to her, he saw Debra making that note on her tablet. She was probably also making a note to check in on Jessica, his very next thought. Mason's servant would have their daughter with them, explaining her absence from the meeting, and Debra knew Brian would want to review the health of both mother and child.

She anticipated his every need. Whereas he...ignored hers.

"Lord Daegan has a situation in Oregon," Lyssa said, breaking into his thoughts. "A full servant that needs to be unmarked before he terminates her Master."

Brian tuned in to the discussion, admonishing himself to concentrate. Regardless, he found himself staying particularly aware of Debra, the lingering musk of her arousal, a combination of her climax and his she hadn't had time to clean from between her legs. Every male in the chamber would know he'd taken her recently, and he didn't mind the feeling at all. Maybe he was going through some type of hormonal surge for young male vampires. Or maybe he was just suddenly noticing what was his and reacting to that.

Fortunately he was a very good at multitasking. He recommended that Daegan bring the marked servant to the research facility. That way he could ensure the proper dosage and compound would be administered to reverse the marking effects and erase the human's memory. At Lyssa's nod, closing the matter, he proceeded from there into an update about the fertility research, as well as current Delilah virus victims.

Unfortunately the cure still required the death of the servant to heal the vampire, something he and Debra were working to change, though so far without much success. In every case but one, the servant had willingly taken the death sentence to protect the Master or Mistress, but the loss of such a dedicated servant was something everyone agreed the vampire in question would welcome the chance to avoid.

Yet they all refused to address the layers of meaning to such selfless devotion.

When he deferred a follow-up question to Debra, he watched her respond in her usual calm manner. Noting the Council's attentiveness, he realized they had as much confidence in her answers as they did his. She'd earned that, tenfold. But if she had to die to save his life, she would, wouldn't she? There was no other logical solution. If the vampire died of the virus, the servant died as well, so the servant being the channel for the serum meant only one life was lost. And there were only about 5000 vampires in a world overrun by humans.

But could life really be quantified that way? There might be billions of humans, but there was only one Debra. As he skimmed the faces in the chamber, he knew every vampire in here but one met the indicators of his fertility study regarding an exceptional relationship with their servant. For Lyssa, Daegan and Mason, there was only one Jacob, Gideon or Jessica. Uthe was fond of his female servant, but he had the more traditional relationship with her.

"Very good." Lyssa nodded. "Mason, Uthe, if you have nothing further…?"

They shook their heads and she addressed Brian. "You'll be traveling to Texas at the end of the week, won't you, Lord Brian?"

"Yes, my lady. There's a made vampire there over three hundred years old. He's agreed to let me interview him and take tissue samples, since he's a prime example of a stable turning. I expect it will only take a couple days."

At her nod and indication that he could take his leave, he gave a slight bow and motioned to Debra. Then, on second thought, he put out a hand, stopping her. "My lady, unless you or the rest of the

Council objects, I will depart a couple days early to make a stop in Tennessee."

"Further research?"

"No, my lady." Brian met Lyssa's gaze. "Debra's grandfather is terminally ill, and I would like to give her the chance to spend some time with him. If circumstances require her to stay a longer time, I will continue on to Texas and pick her up on the way back. Or pay for her airfare to come back when she is ready. By your leave."

Lyssa lifted a shoulder, the light from the room sconces sliding down the wing of her ebony hair. "By your own admission, Debra is as much responsible as yourself for the steps that saved my life not too long ago. You've also indicated she identified the breakthrough variable on the fertility study, a study that may put our birthrate on a more positive track." Lyssa inclined her head. "If she requires a plane ticket to return, and an extended stay with her grandfather, I approve both the expenditure of money and time, and I expect neither Lord Mason nor Uthe will disagree with me."

Uthe made a noncommittal grunt, but Mason straightened from a relaxed panther sprawl in the oversized chair that fit his broad shoulders. The vampire had long auburn hair that framed a strong, arresting face. It meshed with his serious countenance now. "If you feel your presence is required, stay with your servant, Lord Brian," he said. "It sounds like you are well on top of your current efforts."

Brian met Mason's amber eyes. Vampires who achieved the age of those at the Council table had more trouble blending among humans. Not just because of their beauty or the different hue of their eyes, but their exceptional focus and preternatural stillness were harder to mask. Their thoughts and emotions were almost impossible to read, faces often as smooth as a blank slate. Which meant when their expressions were readable, it was deliberate. He saw a clear missive from Mason's.

They serve us, so when it matters, we need to be there for them.

It was a message so at odds with how things had been even five years ago. Everything he'd been experiencing – the nightmares, his interaction with Jacob, what he saw in Debra's mind—was telling him it was time for a vital paradigm shift.

What had Jacob said? Practice what you preach?

As he turned to take his leave, his gaze passed over the male in question, standing behind Lyssa's chair. Jacob's blue eyes flickered with approbation, Brian supposed about his decision to go to Tennessee. Not that he needed a human's approval, but Brian gave the man a nod.

Taking Debra's arm because she looked a little rooted in place, he gave her a nudge toward the door. She jerked into motion, but he could feel she was nonplused as she followed him back to the lab. He heard the flood of thoughts in her head. What just happened? How did he know? Would Jacob have...no, Jacob wouldn't betray my confidence. So he was...listening?

Once in the lab, Brian took a seat on the rolling stool he favored and turned to where she stood uncertainly in the center of the floor. She'd been on firm footing in front of three of the most powerful vampires in the world, yet she felt on quicksand with her own Master. He could fix that. Or enjoy the benefits of keeping her off balance.

"Come here," he said, reaching out a hand.

She came, further bemused by how he grasped her wrist and tugged her between his spread knees.

"Yes, I listened to your mind," he said. He saw how the stern set to his mouth put her on alert. Good. "As far as Jacob betraying your confidence, I agree, he's a good friend who wouldn't do that. But since when do you feel you have the right to keep any secrets from your Master?"

She set her jaw. "I wasn't trying to keep secrets. I just don't want you to have to worry about things like that."

"Like my servant's wellbeing?"

She looked away. "I serve you, my lord. Not the other way around."

When he probed, he discovered she'd literally built a wall around those feelings, thick as the scar on a badly mended heart, protecting an area he hadn't visited in quite a while. The woman who'd been willing to go into a rogue vampire lair, risking torture and death, was terrified of taking this step again, when he'd set her back on her heels so harshly last time. That wall was in the center of those dark places he'd waded through the day before, like a castle with a poisoned moat, affecting everything around it, making the despair grow.

As a result of that realization, he had to rein back his compulsion to hammer at that wall, bring it down. It didn't take a scientist to realize that wasn't the best approach. She'd built it over time; it would take time to bring it down, draw out the poison, so her heart could beat and feel freely again.

So he was going to do something he rarely did. Let his feelings lead him. Standing in a room with the world's most powerful vampires, seeing how most of them felt about their own servants, he felt a new, refreshing determination to try something different from what he'd been raised to do.

"You serve me very well, Debra. Your generosity of spirit and submission run so deep, you make it entirely possible for your Master to be a bastard of the first order."

Her gaze snapped up to him. "My lord—"

He shook his head, stopping her. "We'll deal with the generosity of spirit later. The submission has been a bit of an unfilled well of late, hasn't it?"

Her brow knitted. Curving his hands over her hips, then sliding down to grip her lovely backside, he brought her even closer. As he kneaded, enjoying the pleasure of fondling his servant and how she responded to his touch, he spoke in her mind.

When I spanked you yesterday, your mind opened up. I've been depriving myself of that well, splashing around in the shallows. You need to feel the strength of your Master's will more often. And his hand.

She looked confused, but her body was responding to his touch. As was her pounding heart. She didn't know how to respond, since *Yes, Master* might seem self-serving. He liked confounding that sharp mind. Not to diminish it, but to see what other things came forth when she gave herself to sensation and pure feeling.

"Mason is right. We're at a good place on our ongoing projects." He gave her a leisurely perusal. "So tonight we stop at midnight. I'm in the mood for stargazing on the south lawn, where we can see the moon rise. It will be a warm night. I want you to wear sheer white lace panties and that low cut bra that goes with them. Put on your highest heels, as well as your lab coat. Leave it open." He threaded her pony tail through his fingers. "Leave your hair down. You don't wear it that way often enough. That will change."

"Yes, my lord."

He touched her chin, made her lift her wary gaze to his. "I may be your lord, but there's one thing I am that belongs to you alone, Debra. It pleases me when you call me by that name."

"Master." It came out a whisper and he nodded, restraining the overwhelming urge just to take her right then and there. He wanted to drive up her anticipation, help her knock a layer off that wall he'd forced her to build. He could feel her fear as much as her anticipation, and it curdled in his gut, the things it told him about her...and himself.

"Good." He stepped back. "Let's get to work then."

Chapter Four

Debra spent the early evening dealing with mixed emotions, as well as grappling with the shocking idea that Brian was randomly listening to her mind. But that wasn't the only thing he did that kept her in a distracted state. As he went back and forth between workstations, several times he detoured to where she sat at her desk. He nudged her hair aside, kissed her throat, his hands at her waist coming up to casually cup her breasts, stroke. As he did, he asked how her data was going, solicited feedback from her. Sometimes he just put his hands on her shoulders, kneaded the tight muscles there and in her neck. The sexual undercurrent was there, but it was fueled by the intimacy, rather than him actively trying to arouse her.

When he asked her to get them a candy bar at ten, he took a bite of the snack from her fingertips, nipping them lightly. After she took the candy back to her desk, she had a couple more bites, but left half of it for later, because he called her back over to him. It wasn't work-related, however, at least not immediately. He brought her close, inhaled her breath, licked a bit of the sugar off her lips.

"You have a sweet tooth, my—Master."

"I do. I should indulge it more often." As he delved deeper, his tongue tasting the chocolate flavor that lingered in her mouth, he leaned against the counter, his arm banded around her waist to keep her steady. When he raised his head, her knees were quivering at the look in his eyes.

"You'll get sick," she managed.

"Maybe. Lady Helga thinks we should assign a much higher priority to vampire digestive issues, especially when it comes to chocolate."

"Of course." Trying to appear casual about all of it, she straightened as he let her go, adjusted her lab coat under his amused gaze. "Coming up with the vampire version of Tums is far more critical than resolving the fertility limitations that could result in species extinction."

His grin warmed her from head to toe. Then he glanced back down at what he was doing. "Can you put that equation up on the board so we can both look at it? Something's not coming out right."

She complied, and he shifted to stand by her side. Her brow creased, the variables arranging themselves in her mind. She could see what concerned him. As he hooked a thumb in her back waistband, hip comfortable against hers, he opened his mind to hers.

"What about that value there?" He pointed. "If we switch that out, replace it as an unknown…"

They sorted and rearranged. At a certain point she couldn't tell which of them was working which part of the problem, but then she stepped forward, using her fingers on the touch screen to eliminate one part and add in other variables as they'd done in their minds.

"Yes." His eyes lighted up. "That's it."

She nodded. "That will remove one of the limiting assumptions. It will make the calculations more complex, but then we'll definitely have better control of the overall study."

"Excellent. We might just have time left over for that Tums development after all."

She chuckled at that, shook her head, and went to attend to the change in her files. As confused as she was, it was the best day she'd spent with him in a while. She felt in sync on every level, not just in the research they were doing.

Then she realized the rest of her candy bar had vanished off the counter. Quick as a shot, she ducked under her desk and caught the small fist about to jam the rest of the candy into an open mouth. "Kane, no," she said sharply.

The born vampire, not much more than a toddler in age, gave her his mother's jade *you-will-die-puny-mortal* stare. Ignoring that, she nevertheless had difficulty wresting it from him. Fortunately, Brian came to her aid. "You are getting to be a strong little cuss," he said, but took the candy out of range. "How many times do we have to tell you that chocolate will make you sick?"

"You ate," Kane said sullenly.

"Yes, a bite. You were about to swallow half of it whole. John?"

As Brian raised his voice, the young man appeared outside the lab door. He'd no doubt followed Kane, but had hung back when he realized Brian was present. When it was just Debra, he usually came right in. She had a great fondness for John. The young man was in lanky adolescence, but he had a maturity and patience far exceeding his age, likely a genetic boon from his grandfather. Elijah Ingram had

the patient steadiness of a stone, and a foundation of compassion and generosity of spirit structured with steely self-discipline. His grandson showed all those burgeoning traits. It made her miss her own grandfather all the more when she was around either one of them, and was another reason she'd bonded with John.

"Sorry about that, sir." John crouched in front of Kane. Studying the chocolate smeared on the little vampire's mouth, he gave him a gimlet eye. "Your daddy is going to whip your butt for sure if he finds out you got hold of that."

"I should have put it away," Debra said.

"No," Brian said. "He knew it was wrong. You don't learn self-control by not testing it. Here." Pulling it off the table, Brian knelt by John and handed it back to Kane. "Take the rest. Eat it. See what happens."

"My lord," John said, surprised, but Brian gave him a sharp look.

The boy subsided, pressing his lips together. Though John was clearly protective of his friend, he didn't sass his elders, human or otherwise. It was respect rather than fear, however, for Debra knew no one on the estate except his grandfather would ever touch a hair on his head. Lady Lyssa's protection was upon the human child as much as that of her own son. Not only were the two children fast companions, it was an oath she'd made to Elijah Ingram when he'd agreed to be majordomo of her estate.

Kane knew he wasn't supposed to be disrespectful to adults, either, so he didn't snatch the bar back like a wild animal. But after he took it, he didn't put it in his mouth right away. Instead, he studied Brian, his green eyes measuring the scientist's intent, thoughts whirling in his busy brain.

If a vampire ate too much human food, they'd feel deathly ill for a day or so. Like seasickness, no amount of vomiting relieved the feeling. The person suffering would wish they were dead, for sure, but death was not the result. Just massive discomfort and, as Helga had noted, there was no aid for vampire indigestion. Most vampires only had to make the mistake once never to repeat it. No matter how many centuries they lived, it was a lesson that never faded from the mind.

While Kane's parents and most of the estate had been trying to keep him from experiencing that, Brian had obviously decided that letting a child touch a hot stove was the best way to learn not to touch it, especially for a child carrying the genetics of two very stubborn people.

But he also had their shrewdness. Kane considered Brian's unsmiling face. "Sick."

"Very sick. But it won't kill you."

"Tastes good," Kane complained.

"Yes, it does. Want to see a way around it?" Brian put out his hand.

After a considering pause, Kane turned over the candy bar. Reaching out, Brian clasped Debra's hand and placed the candy bar against her pulse point, smearing chocolate there. Then he lifted it to his mouth, tasting the sweetness just before he bit into the vein, a light penetration that nevertheless had her fingers curling so they grazed his chin. Brian's lips curved against her flesh. He took a small draught only, then closed the wound, licking the rest of the blood and chocolate off of it.

He nodded to Kane. "Putting a flavor you like over the blood gives it a lasting taste in your mouth. It helps satisfy the urge without eating too much."

He handed back the candy bar. "Beyond the issue of making you sick, it wasn't your candy bar. It was mine."

"On her desk. Servant."

They learn young, Debra thought, trying not to roll her eyes. She saw a similar flash of exasperation on John's face. All the human staff were familiar with vampire arrogance. John could probably vouch firsthand for just how early in life a vampire started cultivating the trait.

Brian gave her a sidelong look. *Vampire arrogance? Even me?*

I didn't mean you, my lord. She wondered if it was possible to pull off an inward version of a poker face.

You're not good at the outward one. I like that about my servant.

He gave her a lingering look, and returned his attention to the child.

"Yes, it was on Debra's desk. But what's on my servant's desk is mine, because she's mine. Right? You take from her, you better be sure you have the permission of her vampire."

She wished he felt that way about vampire social gatherings. Especially when Lord Graham was in attendance. She was already hoping they wouldn't encounter him in Texas, but that was pretty close to his territory. The very thought that he might join them at the Texas overlord's home had her tightening up, but she sent herself a firm admonishment. There was nothing she could do about it. She'd get through it, as she always did when she encountered him.

With a start, she realized she'd drawn Brian's attention. His hazel eyes were suddenly much sharper, suggesting irritation. Anger? Because he'd been talking to Kane, she hadn't expected him to be listening. But even if he was, he didn't usually care about how she managed her solo appearances at vampire gatherings, anyway. He knew she'd handle them appropriately, for she'd proven she could, repeatedly. She tried to think of something to say to address whatever had aggravated him.

Fortunately Kane distracted them both. He handed her back the candy bar with a dignified nod, though he directed his words to her Master. "I apogize, Brin," he said.

Brian's mouth twitched at the solemnly mangled English. "Apology accepted." Then he broke off a small piece of the candy and handed it over. "Remember what I said."

Kane's eyes lighted on John. The boy was already second marked by the young vampire and occasionally offered him blood, though his mother and father were still his primary source for the time being. Jo, a second mark on the estate, also served as his blood nanny when the demands on Lyssa as Council head made regular feedings difficult.

John shook his head vehemently. "Forget it. You're not putting that sticky stuff on me. Let's go find Jo."

As Kane preceded him out of the lab, his stalk a short-legged, less steady version of the haughty sweep his mother had perfected, John gave Debra a hopeful look. "Can I stake him? Just once? You guys could bring him back to life, right?"

Brian chuckled. "Dr. Frankenstein I'm not, John. And I wouldn't advise saying that around Lady Lyssa."

"She threatens his life all the time." John, unimpressed, followed Kane out. A few moments later they heard the boys take off like a charge of cavalry, indulging their favored pastime of striking all the suits of armor on the main hallway that led back to the living quarters of the estate.

Giving her a humorous look, Brian shook his head and turned back to his work on the counter. She studied his back. The nerves in her wrist were still tingling from his lips, her mind whirling at emotions he'd revealed as he delved into her mind. She wasn't sure what was going to happen later tonight, but he had her unbalanced, for certain. She was afraid, anxious, aroused…anticipating. But mostly afraid. Because her heart was considering the impossible.

Brian was gazing into his microscope with that concentrated set to his mouth that always made her want to nibble on his lips. His hip was cocked, hand braced on the edge of the stainless steel counter, a lock of hair falling over his right eye, which was focused as a laser beam on what he was doing. She could almost feel his mind accelerate, the numerous calculations he was considering in that oblivious sexy pose.

Sometimes when she was close to him working, she had the urge to be like Whiskers. The cat was often found in the furnace room, asleep in a flat, furry puddle on top of the machinery. All those complex interior parts working together to produce a heated, humming vibration. She wanted to flatten herself against Brian, just feel him thinking, breathing. The pulse of his heart and mind made her world work, heated her through and through, the way the furnace kept the house warm.

God, she couldn't resist him. That was what scared her most of all. She really had no choice, when it all came down to it. She couldn't survive this attention if it wasn't going to last…if it meant nothing. If it turned out to be another lie.

It was never a lie, Debra.

Her stomach leaped like a frog. He didn't look up from the microscope, but she saw the tension in his shoulders, felt the flash of heat from his mind. She didn't want to follow up on that, didn't think she could. So she turned back to her own work.

§

Brian had been clear. He expected her to wear the lab coat— open—over the lacy bra and panty set. He also told her to wear the one pair of stiletto heels she had.

As she left her room and headed for the south lawn near midnight, she knew she might encounter someone in the hallways, but a servant in a state of undress didn't cause the bat of an eye lash in a vampire enclave. She still wasn't comfortable with it, but fortunately everyone else seemed to be.

As if summoned by that wry thought, the first person she met was Jacob. Though he was obviously headed somewhere, striding with purpose, his step hitched as he got a full view of her, and he detoured from the intersection of the hallway to intercept her.

She was still bad about blushing. Jacob's gaze was coursing over her with not-unpleasant male appreciation and she had to suppress the ridiculous urge to close the lab coat. He'd seen her naked plenty of times. Just not dressed provocatively like this.

"Nice night to go out. You might get a little chilly, though." He was picking on her in that gentle way of his, trying to make her feel less self-conscious. Would she ever figure out how to accept this like the others did? How did they do it?

When Jacob reached out to run a knuckle along her cheek to tease her about her blush, she stepped back, nearly bumping the suit of armor behind her. "Sorry," she stammered. "I can't."

Brian had made something else clear before he left her at her door to prepare. It was a provocative mandate he'd never put upon her before, contributing even more to her unsettled state of mind. She knew she sounded like an idiot, so she cleared her throat, tried to grab hold of the maturity she used to present things to Council. It had been so long since Brian had treated her like this, she was acting like a nervous schoolgirl meeting her crush behind the gym.

"I meant...Lord Brian specified that no male was to touch me on my way to him...like this."

Jacob's shift in expression made her suddenly aware of him as a very sexually confident male, one who had more than a touch of sexual Dominant as well. The submissive in her couldn't help but get flustered by it.

He gave her a nod. "That'd be my move, if you were mine. Atta boy, Brian."

Tossing her a fond look, he stole a quick tug of her hair as he resumed course. Though not technically an infraction, it pushed the edges of it. She gave him an exasperated look and continued on her way, but she did feel a bit steadier.

It was a beautiful night. A full half-moon over the south lawn made the thick grass a pale silver-green. Slipping off her heels, she carried them through the landscaped gardens. Since she always enjoyed the rose arbor and it wasn't out of her way, she took the winding path of stepping stones through it. The fragrance of the blooms clustered so close around her inspired her to stop and take a quick sniff of a light pink one, enjoy the feel of the silk petals against her nose and cheeks.

There's a pair of shears sitting on the bench. Brian spoke in her head. *Clip one off.*

When she hesitated, she heard his velvet chuckle in his head. *I already asked Lyssa if it was all right. We're safe from her wrath.*

She smiled at that. Picking up the shears, she wondered how he'd anticipated her path.

I'm a little more observant than my servant thinks I am.

It was an unnerving thought, one that sent a shivery cascade of feeling through her. Carefully snipping off the bloom, leaving a half foot thorny stem, she put down the shears and brought the blossom back to her nose for another pleasurable inhale.

Trail it between your breasts. Over them.

She did, her breath catching at the sensation and his command. The scent wafted up as nerves tingled along the curves, held up plump and enticing in the bra he'd wanted her to wear. Jacob hadn't been able to look away from them.

I'd advise you not to bring up his name again tonight.

It was an easy command to follow. There was only one name she wanted to think about.

Master.

Slide it lower. Along your thighs.

She put the shoes down and obeyed, making a hum in her throat as the weight of the bloom aroused her clit under the silky panties. It was already engorged and wanting attention.

Then come find me and I will attend to it.

Clasping the rose and reclaiming her shoes, she moved along the stepping stones. Once emerging from the gardens close to the house, her bare feet sunk into a carpet of grass. She was on the main stretch of the south lawn, four acres of lush green dotted with trees and hedge groupings, backed by a thick forest. But a servant always knew where to find her vampire.

On the western corner of the mowed area, a trio of live oaks provided his stargazing spot. A nice flat stretch glided down a slope to a pretty man-made pond with a fountain. The soft rush of water was like the sound of the wind. She saw the silhouettes of the ducks sleeping on the banks, since a mallard pair and their annual crop of babies lived there in the warmer months.

Then she saw Brian, and everything else disappeared.

She did pick at him about his pocket protectors and sweater vests, but he was never rumpled or mismatched—except for the occasional need to straighten his tie as she'd done earlier. When he wore one, he tended to pull at it while working. Otherwise, his clothing was always high quality. He wore slacks and crisply ironed shirts, matched with tailored coats when needed. Inside the lab or out, he looked like a wealthy man, a successful scientist who ran his own facility, ready to present to his benefactors or direct a full lab staff as needed. He didn't really do casual.

Tonight he had. In a way that had her swallowing, hard.

He wore a pair of belted jeans and nothing else. The body she'd enjoyed touching for such a brief time in the bedroom was on mouthwatering display, the sculpted pectorals and tight abs, the shoulders just the right breadth. The jeans weren't tight, but they were worn enough to cling the right way to groin and ass. He was stretched out on a blanket on his side, head propped up on one hand, his body sprawled out like a lazy predator, an impression enhanced by the sharp focus of his eyes, covering her from head to toe.

"Put on the shoes, then come to me," he said.

She'd maneuvered on the four-inch stilettos well enough in the halls. Maybe better than well enough. That pendulum sway to her hips the unstable shoes required had been another thing Ja—those she passed—noticed.

Brian's eyes glinted, acknowledging the wisdom of her self-editorializing. Balancing herself precariously, she put on one shoe, then the other. The only way to walk across the few feet of grass in stilettos would be carefully, on her toes, a mincing gait that made her breasts quiver in a way she could tell he liked. He even pushed himself up on one straightened arm to get a better look. For her part, she couldn't take her eyes off his bare chest, the corded throat, his muscles layered and stretched over his abdomen, drawing the eyes to denim molded around his groin. He was aroused, evident by the sizeable strain in that area. She moistened her lips.

Right before she stumbled.

She'd never been good with the blasted things, even on solid surfaces. For the most part, Brian had always been fine with her wearing modest one- or two-inch heels for Council events or vampire formal occasions to save her embarrassment. As a result, this was the only pair of spiky heels she owned, purchased early in their relationship when she was learning what vampires liked to see their servants wear. When she first wore them, Brian hadn't seemed that intrigued, so she'd put them away.

She expected a face plant in the grass. Instead, she found herself caught against that solid chest, his arms around her as he steadied her, drew her back to an upright position that pressed her lace-clad breasts against his bare skin. He smiled down at her. "Kick them off."

She did. She was average height without them, but right now he felt so much taller.

"Next time I'll have you wear your canvas sneakers," he said. "That old ratty white pair you like so much."

"It wouldn't go so well with this outfit."

"I think it goes perfectly with you." He slid the light coat off her shoulders so she was in bra and panties alone. Then he bent and placed a kiss on her back, below her left shoulder blade.

Directly over her third mark.

The significant, tender and yet possessive gesture made every nerve ending in her body yearn toward that spot, her heart somersaulting. Every full servant bore a mark, a cross between a scar and a birthmark that appeared during the third marking. When he'd fully marked her all those years ago in the lab, her third mark had appeared on her back, positioned over her heart. It looked like an X, with the two top ends thickened.

The shape of the mark was dictated by forces beyond vampire understanding, usually an unmistakable meaning to it. She hadn't yet figured out what hers was, but just having his mark had always been meaningful enough to her.

He brushed his lips over it again. "Sweet servant," he murmured. "Down on the blanket. On your back."

As she complied, he stood over her, watching, and it stole her breath, his arousal prominent against the jeans, his unapologetic virility. It was a side of Brian very few ever saw. This version of it was new to her as well, but entirely welcome.

"I'm glad my servant approves." He gave her a faint smile tinged with sensual warmth, telling her he wasn't chiding her. "Spread your legs for your Master."

She did, and he moved forward, hooking his foot under her right knee and moving it so it bent outward. Understanding, she did the same with the other, so her thighs formed a wide, empty cradle. The position also stretched her panties over her swollen cunt.

"You're nice and wet already."

"Yes, Master. For you."

His gaze flickered up at the uneven sound of her voice. She was trying not to let the emotional interfere, but her heart was starting to race like a freight train. She didn't want to have a panic attack, wanted to live in the moment and not worry about what this did or didn't mean. But she couldn't seem to be objective.

When he stood over her like this, he seemed so much bigger, larger than life. Like when they'd met. But that wasn't why she'd fallen for him. It was when she realized he was a complicated mix that he'd won her heart. He was a genius, yes. He could also lose ten pens a week because he couldn't remember where he'd put them down. He'd break off in mid-conversation with a high-ranking vampire simply because he went somewhere else in his head to solve a problem. Though it didn't happen too often, she'd seen him lose his temper, break the top of a table with his fist. It had been yet another test of the serum cure for the Delilah virus, another failure to find an alternative to killing servants.

She was the one who'd convinced him they needed to take a short break on that project. Give it time to breathe and come back to it. They would find the solution that would save both servant and vampire eventually. She was sure of it.

It had been a while since she'd remembered so vividly that dangerous strength he possessed. He could crush her in his arms, yet she never feared his hold on her. Not for that reason.

She knew he was in her head. She could tell by his changed expression. But he didn't say anything about those thoughts. He was her Master. It wasn't his job to reassure or explain. She embraced that idea, even as the gaps it left felt like open wounds.

He dropped to one knee next to her, leaned down and stroked his fingers through her hair, spreading it out on the blanket. "Your hair has more colors of gold than autumn," he observed. "You never color it."

"No…I never have."

Nodding, he traced her cheek, her lips. "And very rarely do you wear makeup. Sometimes for formal events you add some eye liner, shadow, and it makes your eyes even more soulful. They're like a shy animal's eyes, liquid brown and watchful, wanting to trust."

"Master." *Don't. Please don't.*

His own eyes darkened. "I'll do as I wish, won't I? And you'll bear it."

She nodded, choked out a sob as he bent, put his mouth on hers. Not a penetrating, demanding kiss, but a meeting of lips where he nuzzled, breathed into her mouth. It was terribly unfair, that a man this intelligent could kiss like this.

He lifted his head only the necessary space to stare into her eyes. "You've been wanting to ask me a question this week. I thought I caught a glimpse of it once or twice, but it's surrounded by a lot of emotions. I think we'll both benefit from you being brave enough to walk out of that storm and ask the question."

No. Don't make me go through that again. Please.

He touched her face. "If you know one thing about vampires, you know we have a ruthless side. I'm no exception to that."

No, he wasn't. She closed her eyes. "Please don't make me do it, Master."

"Ask me the question, Debra. Trust me as you did once, long ago."

That brought her eyes back open. While he still had that implacable look, there was something else there. A desire...a hope. Maybe a need for her to trust him.

He hadn't earned that. She knew that, rationally. But the plain truth of it was she'd never been able to deny him anything.

Beyond that, sometimes a project turned up data that provided answers for another project. The Delilah virus cure had required in-depth research on the makeup of the servant himself or herself. As such, it had led to a hypothesis, still under investigation, that vampire servants were humans chemically disposed to being servants. Once in contact with a vampire, the human's irresistible compulsion was to take the path that led to the full marking.

They'd done some preliminary research and found a general marker, but it seemed to have DNA linkages, suggesting many servants might have that compulsion only with vampires of a certain type of compatible anatomy. Chemical proof of soul mates, in a sense.

Remembering that untested hypothesis, as well as his changed behavior this week, the hopes he was trying to unbury inside her, she found the courage to ask the question.

"My lord...Master...did you..." She wet her lips, looked up at the moon. "When you did...what you did, with Lady Carmela, was it because..."

Did she really want an answer to such a painful question?

He slid his arm beneath her, lifting her into a sitting position to put himself behind her, his thighs bracketing her hips. Banding his arm across her chest, he touched his lips to her ear. "Ask it, Debra."

His chest was a comforting firm brace behind her. Her hand fell on his thigh, nails digging in as she curled her other fingers over his forearm. "Was it to protect me?"

"It would make me seem noble and self-sacrificing if I said yes, wouldn't it? You might find it in your heart to forgive me. But you would know that's not the full truth, and I won't let a lie stay between us."

She almost heard her heart crack. She would have done the unthinkable, scrambled away, run back to her room and close the door, but he tightened his arm around her. He wasn't done with her.

I'll never be done with you.

She might die from the pain of that. She was starting to understand all too well why some servants took their lives.

In a heartbeat, she was on her back on the blanket again and he was leaning over her, looking more menacing than she'd ever seen him. A quick look around told her they were still alone, that he wasn't bracing for an attack. Which meant that menace was directed toward her. Her heart skipped a beat as he captured her jaw in a bruising grip. The shadows of the night turned his eyes to storm fire. His fangs had unsheathed.

While Brian suffered from it far less than others, a vampire under the age of a hundred could be goaded to savagery, a loss of impulse control hazardous to everyone within reach. It appeared she had provoked it.

She froze, knowing it wouldn't save her any more than a hapless field mouse, but she couldn't have run from him anyway.

I forbid it, Debra. If even the thought of taking your life crosses your mind...

Her eyes widened at the terrible look on his face. It mattered to him.

"Of course it matters," he snarled. "What kind of monster do you think I am?"

When she flinched, he made a visible effort to rein himself back. He sat back on his heels, but straddled her thigh, his other hand braced alongside her hip, keeping her on her back.

She moistened her lips. "Tell me why you did it. Honestly."

"Except for that night, I've always been honest with you. Haven't I?"

He had. Which was why that night had always held some sense of wrongness, because it felt like he'd lied to her. She'd foolishly clung to the hope Jacob had dangled as to why Brian had done it, but her Master had just taken that slim hope away, denying it was for such a selfless reason. She'd known that anyway. She wasn't stupid. She just had never been able to figure out the whole of it. But would the truth help or make it worse? She tried to stave off the feeling that the ground was crumbling under her feet.

"He wasn't entirely wrong. Just not entirely right." Brian sighed, stroked her jaw, her neck, dropped his touch to the raised curve of one lace-clad breast. Then down even further, trailing along her stomach, a hip bone, the lace of her panties stretched over it. When he slid a fingertip below the edge, she trembled, hating him for being able to make her helpless to his desires when he was tearing her apart inside. His eyes darkened, seeing it, hearing it.

"I am a young vampire," he said quietly. "Even younger then than I am now. I was fighting for credibility among my own kind, espousing ideas many thought were pointless. Vampires are about politics and power struggles, not about working together to solve problems like fertility and sun vulnerabilities. Or a synthetic blood that might make us less dependent on human blood, just in case someone ever comes up with something even more virulent than the Delilah virus. I've always known my desire to research these things weren't idle curiosity, a personal hobby. Born vampires, the base stock for all vampires, are a terribly endangered species. A fragile one, in some ways."

He shook his head. "It was essential, especially because of my age—let alone my outlandish ideas—that I always appear completely detached, objective."

As he spoke, his gaze was sliding over her, an inch at a time it seemed, reminding her how thorough he could be, how detail-oriented. He caressed the other hip bone, making her twitch restlessly. Bending, he kissed her navel, rimmed it with his tongue. She was dying, her throat closed and choking her, heart aching. When she placed her hand on his head to stroke his hair and he turned enough to kiss her palm, she had to choke back another sob.

He lifted his head, met her gaze again. "I'd heard choosing your first full servant is a lot like a first crush. Having a servant to call my own, and one like you…it was a heady mix, such a brilliant woman willing to submit to me, become my servant." A shadow crossed his gaze. "I spoke to others about it. When I described you to them, how impressed I was with you, how much I wanted you, my feelings must have shown. They teased me. Normal hazing, not even unkind really. But I thought my behavior reinforced what they believed, that I was still going through growth spurts, and my scientific pursuits were simply a phase.

"Then you told me you loved me. You asked if I loved you back. An honest question. You weren't even nervous, so clear-eyed and direct. In your world, it simply is, right? Two people fall in love."

Tears trickled out of her eyes and he put his lips to her cheek, capturing one. He cradled the other side of her face, absorbing those tears in his palm.

"It seemed like the test I was waiting for, to prove to them and you that you didn't have that hold on me. I told myself I was teaching you a lesson, but I was teaching myself a lesson as well. Proving I had the self-control to accomplish everything I intended."

His gaze lifted to hers. "I was testing a hypothesis. 'If she hasn't affected my heart, then I can behave as if she doesn't matter. I can hurt her deeply and still continue to see her as my servant, expecting her to be my servant, no matter what I do to her.' I salved my conscience by reminding myself you came into the relationship fully informed."

"Women are known for an appalling lack of self-regard when they fall for a man," she said. She'd meant to sound wry, not bitter, but she knew she failed. The flash of hurt on his face startled her, but then it was gone, replaced by something softer.

"For the next few years, we stayed so busy. I thought you found a way to heal your heart and accept the way things were."

"You proved your hypothesis." She wanted to be anywhere else, but remained rigid under his touch now. He brushed her lips with a thumb.

"No, I didn't," he said softly. "The intensity, how you respond to me, the overwhelming physical pleasure of having you as my servant, made it easy to assume I had. Yet whenever you kneel to me, whenever I hold you in my arms, it's far from simple."

When her brow furrowed, his lip curled, a sign of personal frustration. "It was a fucked-up hypothesis, Debra, because it was based on twisted logic."

Sliding his arms beneath her, he lifted her to her feet, her bare soles sinking into the blanket, cushioned by the layer of grass beneath. He stayed kneeling, his arms banded around her thighs and hips so she had nowhere to put her hands but on his shoulders, her knuckles brushed by the strands of his blond hair.

"Here's the right hypothesis: If I didn't care for you, then I never would have felt the need to do that." Taking her hands, he gripped them tight. His hazel eyes were serious and intent, the way they were when he knew he'd hit the right vein on a research problem. "Here's another one. 'If I truly love you, then I can convince you once more that I am your Master.'"

She blinked. Had he said...love?

"The Master who cherishes and values you. The one who humbly and on his knees"—he glanced down at himself wryly—"begs your forgiveness."

Amazed disbelief flooded her, followed by apprehension. "Master, don't." She tugged at him. "If someone should see..."

He stayed stubbornly in place. "You risked your life for Lord Daegan, for Gideon and Anwyn. You did it without thought."

"I had every intention of waiting in the car."

He gave her a look. "We're not in the lab. Don't correct me."

An unexpected snuffle of laughter caught her. He was right, it was the only place where she would correct him. But when she kept trying to get him back on his feet, he gave her a little shake.

"Cease. I'll do as I like, risk or no risk, because I hurt you badly, Debra. I damaged your trust, and I'm realizing exactly what that may have cost me. Tell me what I can do to earn your forgiveness. Show me."

Dear God, he meant it. Here she was, facing what she'd always hoped to hear from him, yet there were too many layers of hurt. It didn't penetrate. It didn't feel real. How could he really know what it meant if he'd fought it so long? If he'd never really loved? And in his world, he could be risking...everything.

"Yes, I could. But a scientist who ignores truth and how it influences everything else fails anyway." She saw that flash of frustration again. "Debra, I don't deserve your trust. I know that. But give me something. Let me earn at least an ounce of your forgiveness tonight. I want to find the woman I met in that lab long ago, the one I hope I haven't destroyed."

He had destroyed her. But he'd remade her as well, the subsequent years of emotions and experiences crafting a whole new person, a new way of looking of things. Built on the foundation of the Debra she'd been.

She took a breath. If this was a dream, it would be just as capable of breaking her as it would if he didn't really mean it. Because she didn't want to wake from a dream like this.

An ounce of forgiveness. One tiny step. It seemed so little, but his steady expression told her he knew just how wide a chasm it was. She closed her eyes.

He wanted her to show him how he could earn her forgiveness. It was far more likely that he could show *her*. As she bit her lip over that thought, she sensed the warm drift of him in her mind. His feelings so sincere, in a way that had her heart squeezing up into her lungs, inhibiting their airflow.

"You know that's not medically possible."

She opened her eyes. "You're not supposed to correct someone you're asking to forgive you."

"Valid point. I'll file it away for later discussion."

She resisted the urge to pinch him, then glanced down at the blanket. She saw the rose that had fallen there.

"Can you...would you lie on your back, my lord?"

He considered, then nodded, complying. She held her breath, not sure this was really happening as he stretched out on his back for her. He let one arm lie above his head, the other resting loosely across his abdomen. His gaze never left her, making things tremble in her lower belly. Kneeling next to him then, she picked up the rose. The breeze picked up a little, riffling the petals, his hair across his brow, sending another shiver across her skin.

"Put the coat back on if you're cold." His voice, a masculine tenor well suited to presentations and convincing others of his intellectual authority, was potent in a whole different way when lowered to a sensual purr.

She shook her head, then dropped her touch, letting the bloom slide over his chest, his upper abdomen. His gaze shifted, tracking it, and she drew in a pleased breath, seeing his skin shudder under the touch of the flower. She made a circle around his nipple, saw it harden. Leaning forward, she braced herself with a hand curled over his upper thigh, so high her forefinger could make a tentative caress of his testicles under the denim.

"Debra."

"I'm working on forgiveness, my lord. As you commanded."

His lips quirked at that, but then they firmed, his eyes watching her like a hawk watched a field mouse. That waiting intensity told her eventually he would strike, and the pleasure would overwhelm her. Doing what he'd so rarely allowed her to do was overwhelming enough by itself.

It couldn't fix all that buried hurt, no. Trust didn't switch on and off like a light. But he was a smart man. She knew he knew all that. He was asking her to take a step in that direction, see if she could find it in her to open herself to the possibility. She wanted that, she truly did, but she'd learned the heart, when wounded, didn't always respond to the wants of the mind. It had to make its own decision, in its own time. And it wasn't necessarily easy. There were so many pitfalls in the vampire world, so many things that would require Brian to underscore her status as a mere servant, things that could send her back in that wrong direction again. Things beyond both their control.

But he was right. She'd known most of those requirements when she signed up for this. It was how he'd abandoned her emotionally to face so much of it alone that was at issue. He was giving her an opening, a chance to believe he might be capable of making up for it. If she'd lacked any evidence to back that up, she would have been dead in the water right now. But she'd seen the type of vampire master possible in the relationship between Mason and Jessica, Lyssa and Jacob...

It would be new to him, though. He was right, in that all his focus had been proving himself to the vampire world, a world that still pretty much considered her expendable, her needs second to all of theirs. Could she be strong enough to trust him through missteps, even if he was truly headed in the direction she'd hoped for all along?

That she'd sensed during those first few days together, so strongly she'd never doubted his feelings had been real, not all these years. Sometimes that was more painful than finding out she'd deluded herself.

She had no answer to any of that. She'd just focus on this, see if she could navigate a moment of trust. The physical part of it was certainly no hardship. But an edgy part of her wanted to test, to push the boundaries of what had always been acceptable between them. So she let that bloom drift down over the nice muscled ridges of his stomach and play at his belt. It wasn't tight at his lean waist, so she brought her fingers into the equation. Dipping below, she found his bare hip bone and nothing else. No underwear. It made her pulse trip a little faster, thinking of his cock and testicles right against denim.

She reversed the bloom. The stem had several sharp, thick thorns. As she fed the stem below the line of the belt, imagining it curving on the inside of his hip bone, against the tender flesh over the pubis, she saw his gaze sharpen on her again, felt his attention in her mind, like the hum of electricity. She savored feeling him there. Those servants who grumbled about the vampire's presence in their minds didn't know what it was like to do without it. When he was aroused and his emotions were high, it was as clear he was inside her head as if he was standing behind her in the lab, his breath on her neck, making her have to work to concentrate, not mess up her process.

You manage it well. I'll have to work on that. It would be nice to punish you for actual cause sometimes.

He was teasing, because they took the work they did seriously. But she expected there were some less important things she could mess up. Just because.

His lips curved at that. *My servant likes punishment. I'll make a note to meet her needs more often.*

The usual thought crossed her mind, that her needs weren't his to worry about, but he lifted the hand on his abdomen, grazed her cheek. *Everything about you is mine to worry about, Debra. It always has been.*

She ducked her head, not able to handle that. Too close to that nest of snakes that could eat her alive from the inside, if she let herself trust too fast, too much. Bracing both her hands on his hip, over the stem beneath the cloth, she pressed down, hard. Harder.

She felt two of the thorns puncture him. He didn't flinch from the pain, but fire flared in his gaze, all the muscles along that distracting upper body rippling. As she eased off, small spots of blood bloomed through the fabric, staining the fibers.

"Blood isn't easy to get out of clothes."

"I don't want it to wash out." She wanted there always to be evidence of this one experience he'd given her. If there wasn't another, maybe having at least one like this would last her the next seven years.

She unbuckled his belt, slid the button of the jeans free to push her hand in beneath the zipper. She guided it down from inside and out to ensure it didn't catch any tender, turgid flesh. There was a difference between intentional pain, like what she'd done with the rose, and pain caused by carelessness.

Perhaps that was why the memory of Lady Carmela had remained so painful, festering. Because he'd done it intentionally. It tempted her to lock down her emotions, simply enjoy the physical the way he'd been doing throughout their relationship, and not risk her emotions. He was right. It was safer that way.

"Debra."

She shook her head, peeled back the jeans. Removing the rose, she dropped it to the blanket and put her mouth over one of the marks, relishing the taste of his blood. Even a few drops could be rejuvenating to a servant, and it fizzed through her, making her leave off the delicate licks and suck on his skin instead, swirling over it with the tip of her tongue. Her hand slid down to cover his erection, stretching up thick and tempting out of the open jeans. He pushed up into her hand, his breath drawing in, part growl, part sound of pleasure. She didn't have to imagine the restraint he was exercising, letting her do this. She could feel it, like a chain stretched to breaking.

Often after a vampire social event, once the vampires turned in for the dawn, the servants would have impromptu gatherings of their own, if they were friendly enough with one another. She remembered one where Dev, the Australian bushman who was Lady Daniela's servant, had made them all breakfast as they lounged about the kitchen. During the gossip and information trade that was part of such an informal social meet, one servant had speculated whether or not there were any submissive vampires. It was intended as a joke, and had gotten the expected eye rolls and chuckles.

There were always exceptions in Nature. It was one of the ways life evolved and adapted, but for Brian it wasn't a remote possibility.

Other vampires might think him mild-mannered because he didn't care about pissing contests at fancy vampire dinners, or political wranglings at the Council table. But he was passionate and determined about his work, single-minded in a way no different from Daegan Rei studying a target, or Lady Lyssa facing down the entire Council.

Lord Uthe once said I wouldn't be the one at the head of the army, storming the castle. I'd be the engineer, tunneling beneath to bring the whole thing crashing down.

She smiled at the thought. *I believe that was Lord Uthe's version of a compliment.*

But she agreed with Uthe's point. When Brian had his mind made up about something, he wouldn't let any obstacle stand in his way. Just like now.

His hand slid to her hair, tangled there. Making clear he'd given her as much license as he would tolerate, he grasped his cock with his other hand, using his hold on her hair to direct her mouth elsewhere. She didn't resist, eager to take him into the back of her throat as she'd learned to do, wanting to give him pleasure. Her body vibrated with that need.

Reveling in the strength and demand communicated by his grip, she was surprised when he lifted her off him after mere moments and had her straddle him, shoving his jeans down. He didn't thrust inside her, though. He sat her on his engorged cock, its length splitting the folds of her sex as he cupped her breasts, thumbs sliding in the cleavage while he molded and kneaded. Releasing the front clasp of the bra, he pulled the garment off her shoulders, but only to tangle it around her wrists, tighten it behind her back before he reared up and clasped both her breasts again, bending his head to tease, lick and suckle her. When she arched backward, moaning, he dropped a hand to support her back, let her lean against his strength, fingertips playing in her hair, which fell past her shoulder blades and into his grasp with her head tipped back. He scored her nipple with a fang, earning a gasp and a more severe arch. His pleased, throaty chuckle told her he liked her response.

He slid his touch between her bound wrists and her body to play in the cleft beneath the panties. When he tore the garment, yanking it out of the way, the impulsive gesture startled and aroused her further. He gripped her buttock, showing her he wanted her to move against his cock, rub her soaked crotch against his length. She complied, her mind now following his will, needing, wanting nothing else than to be his to command.

Sweet servant. Beautiful Debra. Dance for me.

As she rotated her hips on him, her body undulating, he was using his mouth on her again, making his way up her sternum. She had her head tilted fully back when he bit, taking a draught of the blood she alone would give him. She knew he never drank from any other.

Of course. You're my servant. Your blood is mine alone. All of you is mine.

The surge of emotional pain was far more agonizing than any physical pain he could give her, but as she stiffened, he caught her head in both hands, cradled her face, made her look at him.

"We're going to figure this out, Debra," he said fiercely. "I know it won't happen immediately, but you will give me all of it. Your pain, your sadness, your tears. I've been ignoring the best part of our bond. Your heart and soul are mine to explore as well."

As he held her gaze, she felt it, that link they shared, three marks to bind a human soul to a vampire forever. But rather than staying at the level he always did, he started to descend further inside her.

The mind was the repository for any emotions ascribed to the heart and soul. So science said. Yet she thought she was going to have to revise that assertion as she felt her heart start thudding, feeling…something closing around it. Beyond that, her awareness of herself, of everything she was, her entire existence, now shared space with him, a rushing, swirling feeling that filled her core, from her head to the soles of her feet and everything in between, including heart and soul.

It frightened her, and fear turned the feeling into an invasion. He stroked her upper arms, his voice a soothing murmur as he brushed his lips over hers.

"Easy. You've nothing to fear."

She had everything to fear. He'd always left her heart and soul to herself, let her nurse the pains and disappointments there unmolested. Yet as his consciousness wound its way through those dark shadows and locked boxes, it entered them easily. He could see every emotion and need, every craving she couldn't hide from him. How much she needed him, wanted him. How she couldn't breathe without him.

She really couldn't exist without him, even if he broke her heart a million times over. She did hate him sometimes, for what he'd done to her. But her hate wasn't a drop in the bucket next to how much she loved and needed him.

Brian lifted his head, his countenance vibrant with emotions of his own. Shock... speculation. She couldn't invade his mind, couldn't know what he was thinking. Whereas she was stripped raw. Nowhere to hide.

Panicked, she struggled against the restraint on her wrists. He reversed their positions, putting her under him, freeing her hands with a swift movement so they weren't uncomfortably beneath her. Since he still had her pinned with his body, she struck at him, the reaction of a cornered animal, not a rational woman, but he didn't block her. He slid inside of her, invading her in a different, no less devastating way.

He was always a good fit, filling her deep and stretching her, but tasting his blood and touching him as she wished had obviously had an effect, making him even larger than usual. Her cunt clamped down on him in needy response, even as she kept shoving at him, afraid of her feelings.

"Debra, stop." The quiet words were an unmistakable command, but she couldn't. As quickly as she'd had that reaction, it reversed so she had her arms wrapped around him as tightly as she could, pulling him against her so her face was pressed into his neck, legs wrapped over his bare hips. Maybe if she held him so close, as if they were one person, she wouldn't be so afraid.

"Ssshhh." He stroked her hair, mixing it up with little tugs that sent searing jolts through her agitated body. At the same time he settled into an easy, rocking boat rhythm, hips lifting and lowering in smooth thrusts. "I'm here. Trust me. Just trust me for tonight. One step at a time."

He was still at that subterranean level of her mind, at the same time he was physically deep inside her body, and now it was like he was dancing with her emotions, a smooth waltz, inviting her to twine and tangle with his thoughts.

Vampires weren't inclined to reveal their deepest feelings, even to their servants, but he gave her a glimpse of what he felt for her. A flickering starlit sky where there were so many things to explore, three hundred years wouldn't be enough.

She caught another sob in her throat, held him even tighter.

We will take the journey together, Debra. Just be patient with me. I'm learning, the same as you.

He tilted her head back, studied her with an edged look.

"But you'll promise me one thing. You won't take your life. Not ever. And if ever you're thinking of it, you will come to me." His mouth became a thin line. "Though you shouldn't have to. I don't plan to be that far from your thoughts ever again."

Chapter Five

Lyssa had three planes at her disposal as Council Head, and she always generously allowed Brian to use one for his research trips, so he could make the most efficient use of his time. For vampires, travel had a limitation of dusk to dawn, though Lyssa had wisely equipped the planes with an emergency compartment shut off from all light and surrounded with a layer of earth on all sides but the small opening. While nothing above ground during daylight was comfortable for a young vampire like Brian, if needed he could survive a flight through daylight relatively unscathed. This trip was fortunately not one of those times, since the flight from Atlanta to Tennessee wouldn't take that long.

Debra sat in the cushioned seat which she knew could be reclined for napping if needed. She resisted the urge to review her notes on their Texas subject. Caleb "Butch" Buford Dorn had been made by Diego Santos three hundred years ago, when the rules about making a vampire had been far looser. However, Diego had shown a responsible, common sense awareness of the principles that later became law. Debra had interviewed him in Barcelona prior to scheduling the meet with Butch. Diego had ensured he had Butch's consent, but even before that, he'd determined the man had a strong physical constitution, matched with an equally strong will, likely to survive and eventually master the impulse problems and physical instability that plagued poorly chosen made vampires.

However, the reason Brian and Debra had such a keen interest in Butch was that he'd shown remarkable stability at a young age. He was turned at thirty-eight, so Brian had theorized that maturity might be a factor, since the percentages of made vampires ruled too unstable to be allowed to survive, or who were unable to overcome blood hunger and violent impulses in the expected timeframe, tended to be younger when they were turned.

Brian had been an exception like Butch, only on the born vampire side of the equation. Throughout their handful of years together, Debra had gleaned everything she could about her Master's childhood and early years. He'd been capable of extraordinary self-control, managing the volatility that kept most vampires at their sire's side for several decades. His father had deemed him ready to attend college on his own to get his first master's degree when he was twenty-seven. She'd met his father once or twice on their visits to England, and found him an austere and entirely intimidating male, a powerful vampire who'd been considered for Council leadership but had turned it down, preferring his role as Region Master of the UK.

During that first visit, Brian's father had brought her into his study by herself. He'd had her stand before him for forty-two minutes without saying anything. Even though her gaze remained lowered, she never felt his eyes leave her. Debra worked through equations in her head, went through the periodic table, named all the muscles and bones in the body, but she never flinched or shifted. After that time period, he'd spoken.

"Will you take care of my son, Debra?"

"I will, my lord." Now she lifted her gaze, met his. "I do."

He nodded. "You may return to your duties."

Butch's historical data indicated he'd overcome his bloodlust urges by sixty-two, only twenty-four years into being a vampire, such that Diego had felt comfortable giving him rein to pursue his life and accomplishments. By the first century mark, Butch had already made a fortune through various pursuits, and now he had an enormous cattle spread in Texas. He'd also been named overlord of that vast state. Made vampires rarely became overlords, and almost none made the Region Master level. Butch might well be the next to claim that distinction.

Debra glanced up as Brian's foot brushed hers. It was an incidental contact, because he was scribbling furiously on a pad, crosschecking something on his laptop. As she watched, he shoved impatiently at the hair that fell over his forehead. He'd cut it short once, like a military cut. She hadn't liked it that way, but she hadn't said anything.

You didn't need to. I could tell.

His gaze lifted to her briefly, then he went back to his figuring.

So he'd changed it. For her? She loved running her fingers through the strands, so she wasn't complaining. She just couldn't imagine that he'd done such a thing for his servant.

Your Master is a selfish bastard. He likes it when you touch his hair. It was entirely self-interest. Now go back to your work. You're distracting him.

He didn't look up, but the comment startled a small chuckle out of her, warmth curling low in her stomach.

Since the night on the south lawn, they'd worked together as they always did, but he was in her mind far more often, just as he'd promised. When he retired for the dawn, if she still had things to do in the lab, he spent about a half hour speaking in her mind before he fell asleep. They talked over data, yes, but they'd also…chat. He'd ask her what she was going to do with her day.

The first time he asked, she rattled off all the work she'd be doing, assuming he was checking to see what her progress would be by the time he woke. When she was done, she felt the caress of his mind like a touch on her skin.

All right. But starting today and every day going forward, you'll take a two hour break away from the lab. Spend time with other servants, read a book in the garden—something not about work. Take a walk. Go swim in the pool with John when he gets home from school. I want you to start taking two hours for yourself, and getting three hours of sleep each day. Five hours total.

He'd cleverly anticipated her overlapping them, the infuriating man.

And I'll be asking what you did with your two hours each day when I wake.

She was going to protest, tell him she couldn't possibly get everything done that he expected her to have done with five hours of down time.

Those are your expectations. Not mine. Before she could feel taken aback by that brusque statement, he added, You exceed mine with barely two-thirds of what you get done. So obey your Master. Two hour break, three hours of sleep.

The first time Jacob had come upon her and John having a splashing contest in the pool, she'd laughed at his look of shock, surprising herself at how good the spontaneous reaction felt. It had been a while since she'd done that.

Jacob had noted her pale skin was reddening in the sunlight. Her third mark healing abilities took care of that quickly after some mild discomfort, but Brian had read the memory from her mind and exhorted her not to go out without sunscreen in the future. Since he'd followed up the admonishment with a quick spanking that left her aroused and trembling, it had crossed her mind to forget more often to earn more punishment. A flash in his eyes and he'd pounced on her in retaliation. After tying her spread-eagle on his bed, he put his mouth between her legs, only allowing her to climax when she was begging, in tears and promising to put on the sunscreen as if she was making a sacred oath to protect the world.

"Lord Brian, we're beginning our approach." The pilot's voice came over the intercom. "We should be on the ground in a few minutes."

To cover the sudden tightness in her stomach, she began packing up her work. She hadn't reached out and called her grandmother, told her they were coming. Though Brian had agreed to do this during the Council update, she'd expected something to come up he'd consider higher priority. She hadn't wanted to raise Grandma's expectations and then be a no-show.

"Thank you." Brian released the button to respond. Usually he would work until the wheels were on the ground, so Debra was surprised to see him pack up the laptop and his notes before he turned his attention to her.

"Are you all right?"

It was an odd question for a vampire to ask, since he could see it well enough in her mind, but he'd done that more often this past week as well. The concern and attentiveness it demonstrated moved her more than was wise.

She nodded, even as she wondered if the real reason she hadn't called her grandmother was to leave herself an out. Even as she longed to see him, some part of her wanted to remember Grandpa as she always had. She wanted to touch his big, callused hand, hear his gravelly voice. He'd been a smoker as long as she could remember, yet it wasn't lung cancer that was getting him, but heart disease. A bitter irony, because he had one of the biggest hearts she knew.

She remembered him gesturing at her with one of his cigarettes before jamming it back in the corner of his mouth, holding it clamped there as they worked on a weather project for her science class. "The will is the most persistent and pernicious part of being human." He snorted out a harsh laugh. "It's why the whole Garden of Eden of story revolves around it. I know these things will kill me, but I'm going to smoke them, despite all that. There's no understanding the will. Sometimes I expect it's the part of us most like God. Hard to understand, but as inevitable as sunlight and rain."

Since she was then at the age when youth questioned everything, she'd told him a scientific person couldn't truly believe in God. He'd given her an indulgent look. "Consider this, little thinker. You can learn everything about painting that Vincent Van Gogh knew. Break it down to brush strokes and paint composition, and you still can't paint like him. You could program a computer to do an exact replica, but you're still copying what he created from something inside him no one can explain." He pointed a finger at her chest, her heart. "The world is four parts science and one part God. As you live and grow, you figure out that one part makes all the rest possible."

He'd given her intellect and faith. Both had kept her at Brian's side, through the good and the bad. As a result, she now understood her grandfather's last comment that day all the more.

More important, that one part is what makes everything else worth living and enduring.

He sounds like someone I would admire.

She looked up, saw Brian studying her again. Rising, he came to sit by her, offering her the handkerchief from the breast pocket of his jacket.

"Oh. Sorry." Mortified, she mopped at the tears.

"Nothing to be sorry for," he said gently. He slid an arm around her, even as she tried to recover her composure.

"I didn't mean to interrupt your work," she said. "You had a good fifteen minutes left." He could do more in fifteen minutes than most could in three days, his mind as quick as his vampire speed.

"I'm at a good stopping place. You should have let your grandmother know you're coming."

"I know." She fiddled with the handkerchief. "Sometimes it's easier not to give them time to think, prepare questions."

"And she might have called your parents."

Debra nodded. She couldn't bear to say good-bye to them again. She hadn't been as close to them as she was to her grandfather, but they were her parents, and they loved her. She wrote regularly, did video chats with them, but she'd weaned them off to less and less. Seeing the confused disappointment in her mother's eyes when Debra made this and that excuse for not visiting, even on holidays, had become excruciating.

"I guess it's time to do it. In another few years it's going to be obvious I'm not aging. Maybe we'll do it after…Grandpa." *Fake my death.*

She couldn't handle voicing it, any more than she could say aloud the reality her grandfather faced now.

§

Brian sat silently, letting her struggle with her thoughts, even though he stayed close to them, making sure his mind touch was strong enough for her to feel him there. She leaned into it as a comfort, the same way she leaned against his side.

Vampires understood that servants turned away from an identity of their own to bond with their Master or Mistress. No career achievements, no job except for caring for their vampire. Vampires also knew the problems of dealing with living family members of those servants, and had protocols in place to address it, to protect the vampire world and to sever those ties more cleanly. Faking a death was the most common practice, since vampires didn't live very public lives for the most part.

Yet a vampire typically possessed a certain detachment about the impact of all that on their servant. He wondered if it was similar to the insensitivity that young adults demonstrated when taking the steps toward severing their childhood dependence on their parents, a necessary trait to ensure the future generation was capable of caring for themselves and the species as a whole. But the parents still grieved an empty nest, the child lost to adulthood.

Until recently, most of the vampires with whom Brian brushed shoulders had servants as much as a century old, where those issues had been addressed and were well in the past. The distance that had grown between him and Debra over the past few years had detached him even further from it, but now he saw it under a glaring spotlight. She'd given up her family, her career, to work at his side, to serve him. Who did that? If she'd stayed in the human world, she'd likely be the head of her own facility, perhaps even researching how to slow down diseases like what was taking her grandfather's life now.

Because he was incapable of not tangling up his personal ruminations with professional ones, he latched onto it as further evidence that chemical makeup determined which humans gravitated toward vampire bonding. Perhaps, when the right circumstances arose "activating" that makeup, it was no more a choice for the human in question than sexual orientation. Vampires were so sexual that gay and straight weren't really relevant classifications for them, but he had to say he definitely preferred women overall. Debra in particular.

He inhaled her scent now, pleased with the mix of fragrances from her soap and shampoo, the touch of rosemary and lavender. Her clean smell made him think of fresh laundry hung out on the line, touched by the sun and wind. When he went with his impulse and nuzzled her hair, he caught her surprised, shy smile. She kept her head ducked down, though, tucking away notes in her computer bag.

Debra didn't fit the profile they'd been building about which humans were predisposed toward becoming vampire servants. Gideon Green was a former vampire hunter who'd reached a crisis point. Jacob had been a drifter of sorts, working with his brother before operating as a Renaissance Faire player. Jessica had been forced to serve another vampire, and was then rescued by Lord Mason. Their circumstances had already divorced them from strong family ties. While they were just a sampling, he wondered how many servants had initially followed career paths with the potential for limelight.

Debra's breakthroughs could easily have brought her widespread recognition, in her field and beyond it. Yet her scientific ambitions were purely service-oriented, also unusual. Ego usually was a key driving factor for one so accomplished in scientific endeavor. He had no doubt his ego and yes, a healthy dose of arrogance, were an essential part of his. But Debra was an extreme submissive, capable of shutting down ego or wellbeing to fulfill her personal markers for service.

Debra had cited the typical servant party line several times, that it wasn't his job to pay attention to her wellbeing. He was the one being served, not the servant. But that was bullshit, wasn't it? There was far more reciprocity to it, as Jacob had stated baldly. If Lady Lyssa, head of the Vampire Council, had figured it out, showing it in ways large and small...

He came out of his absorption at Debra's touch on his knee. Her faint smile didn't dissolve the sadness in her eyes, her drawn look. "What problem were you solving this time?" she asked.

Did she realize there was a slight break in her voice? "The vampire-servant chemical issue. I think I've come up with a new variable. But we'll talk about it later."

He wanted to focus on his particular exception to the rule, on a more personal level. The more time he spent in her mind, the more he realized how much he'd been missing. He surprised her on every level of it when he bent forward, put his other arm under her knees and lifted her onto his lap. "As you said, we have a few minutes before we get in the hangar. Take a nap."

"But…"

Tilting her head back, he kissed her protesting mouth. "No buts. Sleep." He kissed each eyelid closed, then her cheek bones when she tried to open them again, until she was stifling a very un-Debra giggle that made him want to smile, except his heart was too tight, considering the thoughts rolling through his head. "Sleep, servant."

She gave a resigned sigh. "All right, but don't blame me if all this sleeping you want me to do makes us arrive in Texas unprepared."

"Of course I'll blame you. That's why I have you."

"Troll," she said, delighting him. When he pinched her, she nestled her head under his chin, gave a little sigh and subsided.

Maybe it wasn't chemical at all. Maybe humans like her were just a miracle, a once-in-a-lifetime chance he'd fucked up immeasurably because of his misplaced sense of entitlement. He winced at the acid thought, layered with sentiment and guilt, but just because it was driven by his emotions didn't make it a false assumption.

He rubbed her arm, held her. She sank into a fitful doze quickly. She was learning to sleep more often, but he'd had to punish her twice for not watching the time and coming to him at dusk without having obeyed his requirement that she sleep three hours. Though punishment might be the wrong term, since Debra reached a higher level of subspace with a higher level of pain.

He'd been forced—such a chore—his lips twisted wryly—to explore other methods of punishment. Ones that made her more mindful of his orders. Multiple forced climaxes while he had her strapped to a St. Andrews' Cross in Lyssa's well-equipped dungeon had depleted her to the point she slept six hours and lost half a day. Then there was depriving her of a climax entirely. That one had made it difficult for her to sleep at all, but he'd made her stay in the bed with him until dusk that day, not allowing her to entertain herself except to document her sexual fantasies on paper until he roused. Then he made her masturbate herself to climax while he watched. She came within seconds, while he read what she'd written with exaggerated detachment. He'd tossed it aside, remarking on how erratic the handwriting had looked, and then taken her thoroughly, a pleasurable way to start the day.

The more he did, the more he wanted to do with her. He wondered if by stifling it in their earlier years, he'd only delayed the overload of passion a vampire felt when he first took a servant. This past week, the thought had set off several new wrestling matches between his previous thinking and the current hypothesis he was pursuing with her, but so far the latter kept coming out on top. He was actually thinking of expanding their "off time". They both deserved at least one night a week where they did nothing. Enjoyed other pastimes. Since the research facility had been established by Council, he'd been so intent on proving himself worthy of their confidence, he'd driven himself and Debra seven days a week, grabbing leisure time as a guilty snack, not as a full course, leisurely meal.

Maybe on the way back, they'd take a side trip. Not far off course; he wasn't going to presume too much on Lady Lyssa's generosity. However, he could take Debra to some place where they could just spend a night. Maybe Memphis. He expected she'd enjoy watching the evening duck walk at the Peabody. He imagined her standing on the roof outside the duck's grand enclosure, her hair rippling in the strong night breezes while she spoke gently to the birds. She loved animals.

She also loved him. That was something most high-born vampires didn't think much about either, more concerned with obedience and service. Some vampires even deemed it a detriment for the servant to feel too much. His father was certainly that way. He'd approved of Debra, said she seemed logical and controlled.

She could be. But she could also be something else entirely, a wealth of female emotion and yearnings as compelling to him as her sexual and scientific sides. He wanted to push her even further in that direction, see what they could experience if they both went down the road he was beginning to feel they should have explored years ago.

But to get as far down that road as he suspected they both wanted to go, he had to win back her trust. The one thing that couldn't be commanded from a servant.

§

They pulled up to the house at eleven o'clock. Debra had called her grandmother on the way. She'd told Brian the older woman tended to be a night owl, so it was no surprise when she answered on the second ring. Debra explained that they were on an unexpected layover, and asked if she could come by. Though her grandmother seemed surprised and a little stiff, Brian's impression through Debra's mind, she told them to come.

Her stiffness made sense. Her granddaughter, who'd been so close to her grandfather, hadn't seen him in over four years. Brian recalled her last visit with him had been no more than a quick drive to the small Tennessee town when they were in Nashville. She'd done it during the day, after getting his permission. He'd told her as long as she had so-n-so stats ready by Friday, that was fine. Remembering it now, he winced at his callousness. Having those particular stats ready by Friday meant that she'd had to make it a pretty short visit.

And he wondered why she was always exhausted.

He knew the stereotype, that research scientists were oblivious to the world and people around them. The accomplished ones were often self-centered egomaniacs. He'd just never realized how very much he fit the mold. It was an uncomfortable mirror that even his vampire blood couldn't prevent him from seeing.

Jed Sheldon, Debra's grandfather, lived with his wife in a modest brick house on a twenty-acre property populated with woods, unused cow pastures, ponds and several large outbuildings. The buildings had been dedicated to various inventions, if the littering of rusty metal contraptions and other discarded building materials around them were any indication.

As their limo drove up to the house, Vivian opened the front door. The porch light bounced off some of those inventions, transforming them into bizarre lawn art. Debra stared through the tinted window of the car, and Brian gave her cold hand a squeeze. "Why don't you go on up and I'll follow in a couple minutes? Give you two a chance to say hello without a stranger at your back. Though if you prefer, I'll walk up with you."

Her hand tightened on his. Her immediate reaction was: *Yes. Don't make me do this alone.* Then her shoulders squared. She ran through the scenarios, knew his suggestion was the best idea, given her grandmother's potential state of mind.

His surge of protectiveness surprised him. He wanted to correct himself, override her. But he figured out the middle ground. "I'll be right behind you," he promised. *And you know I'm as close as the nearest thought.*

She nodded, her hand still tight on his. Then the driver of the rental car opened the door and she let him go.

Brian waved him away, letting him return to the front seat as he watched out the open door. He didn't know what he'd do if Vivian treated Debra cruelly. He and Debra both understood why she might react with hostility, but still…

Yet when Debra hit the top stair, he saw it wasn't an issue. Vivian already had tears on her face, and Debra didn't hesitate, putting her arms around her grandmother so they could cry together.

"I'm so sorry I haven't been here," he heard Debra whisper. "I think of you every day."

His father had dispensed plenty of advice when Brian told him he was going to make Debra his first personally chosen full servant. *Stay out of their transition from their old life, son. It doesn't concern us, and it's part of how they grow strong enough to serve us three hundred years.*

Brian remembered Debra weeping in the garden. Her desire to sleep and never wake, even as she curled her naked body up next to his like a trusting kitten.

Fuck that.

He left the car, but since Debra and her grandmother were still holding onto one another, exchanging murmurs, he paused in the shadows. Reaching out to one of the discarded inventions, he made the propellers rotate. It looked like some type of all-terrain vehicle that might run on windmill power. Another contraption seemed to be a modified vending machine. Jed's joy in taking mundane things apart only to put them together into something better was a trait his granddaughter had as well.

Maybe he was one of those things.

By the time he approached the door, he'd given both women time to pull themselves together. Debra turned, still holding onto her grandmother. "Grandma, this is Lo—Dr. Brian Morris. I've told you about him."

The fast flash of background in her mind was that she worked with him, that he was a close colleague. Like most human females, Vivian did a double take when she got a look at him in the beam of the porch light. Being excessively attractive was something vampires took in stride. It meant nothing, just a simple genetic fact and a useful tool for spontaneous feeding needs.

As he took her hand with great courtesy, he noted it felt frail and tired. She looked like a woman pushing herself to the edge to care for a dying husband. But she nodded. "Come in. I told Jed you were coming."

She turned her gaze back to Debra. "I haven't seen him so excited in a long time. But remember, his energy comes in bursts. He's likely to nod off on you, but he'll wake again within a few minutes sometimes. I don't want him to sleep through your whole visit, but..."

"I won't tire him out," Debra promised.

They stepped into a neat, comfortable house, the interior décor reflecting accents and colors reminiscent of homes decades ago. Brian often found the offices and homes of older scientists more comfortable to him for that reason. It was probably why he hadn't changed his mode of dress much since the 1950s, despite Debra's teasing.

She'd seemed quite taken with his choice of jeans for the stargazing, though. He'd remember that in the future.

"I made both tea and coffee," Vivian was saying. "There's some coffee cake that Deloris Willoughby brought by yesterday. He changes what he'll eat day to day. He had a few bites of it, but..." Vivian lifted a shoulder. Her chin trembled as she met Debra's gaze, then she closed her hand over hers. "Go in and see him, child."

Debra glanced at Brian.

I'll be right here. If you need me, you just reach out. But take as long as you need. Don't worry about the time. He's your grandfather.

She nodded. Squaring her shoulders, she turned and moved down the hallway

Vivian watched her go, then turned to Brian. Before she could speak, Brian gestured. "I have some work I can do, Mrs. Sheldon. It's late and I have no intentions of making you play hostess when you already have your hands full with so much else. If you wish to join her, please feel free to do so."

It made her smile, an obvious effort despite being genuine. "You're very kind. If you don't mind, I'll do just that. It's been so long since they've seen one another..."

"Please." He sat down, drew his handheld out of his coat, as if he were preparing to work. "Let me know if either of you need anything."

"Thank you." He could feel her eyes on him, then she disappeared down the hall.

As soon as she did, he put the handheld back in his coat and himself in Debra's mind fully. There was no way he'd be more than a breath away while she dealt with this. Truth, since the night under the live oaks, there were times he'd had difficulty pulling out at all, as if Debra were a book he'd had in his possession for some time, one he hadn't read in far too long. Remembering how much he'd enjoyed the first few chapters, he wondered that he'd deprived himself of the rest of the story.

§

Debra sank down next to her grandfather. He was in a hospital bed, the full-sized bed gone to make room for it in their bedroom. A sofa in the corner bore a neatly folded pile of linens. She was sure that was where her grandmother was sleeping. Jed was so thin, half the size she remembered him. He was a tall man with handsome silver hair, a long face that could smile and crease like a wise, good-natured basset hound. Knowing his resemblance to that particular breed of canine, he'd sometimes bay like one, just to aggravate her grandmother.

Debra curled her hand over his, nearly losing herself to tears again when his long fingers twined with hers. She was crying far more than she ever had these past few days, but there was certainly good cause here. He smelled like sickness, like death. She supposed everyone around a dying family member detected those scents, but to a third mark with enhanced senses, it was almost overwhelming, the emotional and physical impact of it.

She focused on his brown eyes, the same color as hers. "Hi, Grandpa."

"Little thinker. Still thinking too much." Letting go of her hand, he brushed a fingertip over the creases in her brow. "Anything come from that thinking? Make anything better?"

"Yes," she said honestly. "I'm helping...people. And learning so much every day. Learning how much I have to learn."

"That's the way of it. It never ends. Just this morning, I thought of the best mousetrap yet. Think Otto would go for it?"

For all the years she'd known him, her grandfather had always had mice. Usually one sleeping in his pocket, or riding his shoulder, taking tidbits from him. There were always a few in the barn, helping with his inventions. Otto was one of the first she remembered.

"As long as it has cheese. And doesn't pinch any of his legs. Or catches his tail."

"Yeah. He never forgave me for that one." Her grandfather chuckled.

"I have my own Ottos. Emilie, Nicolai and Albert." She told him about the maze of tubes, how the children had helped her. She explained John and Kane as offspring of people who worked in the building next to the lab. Like all servants who had to deal with the human world, she was practiced at generalities that gave partial truths. Her grandfather listened, asked her questions about her work. He was far less lucid than he would have been in a stronger state. But she held his hand, told him about the high level research that went into the Delilah virus, framing it in a human context.

"Things like that should be on the TV as big news." He scowled. "Instead of which idiot actor is getting out of rehab or showing her unmentionables to the whole world."

She squeezed his hand, and he chuckled tiredly. "Doesn't matter to me anymore, though. Don't care a thing about watching the news. My time is coming, little thinker."

Her throat closed up. "I don't want you to go. I don't want you to die."

"None of us want to die. But it happens." He studied her. "This 'colleague', Brian Morris. Tell me about him. Is he good to my girl?"

"He's…" Was he good to her? Yes and no. He wasn't required to be. But lately…her thinking was changing on that. She'd always hoped and dreamed he'd want to be good to her, cherish her the way she cherished him.

As her grandfather's brow drew down ominously, she had the alarming impression he might just pull himself right off the mattress even in his weakened state and go after Brian.

"I've learned so much from him, Grandpa," she said hastily. "I thought you were the smartest man in the universe, that I'd never find anyone half as smart. His mind shines like a diamond."

"Too much to hope I'd never have any competition." He settled back, gave her a wink. "How did you meet?"

She'd told him how they'd met right after it happened, via phone call. But she didn't mind telling him again. She'd read him his favorite book over and over, just to sit here with him.

"He was a friend of the director at the Brown Cancer Center. The director let him come in one night to use the lab. You remember I was in charge of the instruments, and since I was working late anyway—"

"As always," he teased her.

"I was keeping an eye on him." Her lips curved as she remembered. "He didn't look like a scientist. He looked like a movie star playing a scientist. Like Paul Walker or Heath Ledger... Someone who puts on a pair of wire framed glasses to look bookish, but he wasn't wearing glasses."

Her grandfather's brow furrowed, his eyes sharpening on her face through the fog she knew was caused by whatever medications he was taking to keep him comfortable. "Your glasses," he said. "I just noticed. You're not wearing any."

She'd been so self-conscious of them in her youth. Thick, coke bottle lenses because her vision had been so poor. After she'd become Brian's third mark, her vision had become progressively better, such that eventually she'd been able to discard them, though she still kept a pair of readers around when the eyestrain became too much.

"Contacts," she said. "They finally came up with a way to make some strong enough."

He smiled at that, patted her hand. "Now you can't hide how beautiful you are any more. And this Dr. Morris noticed, didn't he? So what happened in the lab that made him realize how wonderful my girl is?"

She shook her head at that, but told him. "I happened to notice some of what he was working on, and we started discussing it. We spent that whole first night in the lab, didn't even realize it until it got close to dawn..."

At his invitation, she worked with Brian three nights straight, helping him extrapolate his data, getting his input on her own research, both of them advancing further as a result. The sexual tension grew as well, incidental brushes growing more significant and lingering as they swapped places at a monitor or in front of a microscope. But along with that tension came a relaxed intimacy she hadn't experienced with any male before. When she ordered her usual Chinese takeout, they talked about a random wealth of topics. He'd declined her offer to order him food, but had taken a bite of dumpling from her hand, his own circling her wrist briefly, caressing her pulse before pulling away.

He'd only restrained himself until the third night, but by then her body was humming with need. In the daylight, when she'd snatched a few hours of sleep at her neglected nearby studio apartment, she'd almost used her hand or vibrator to give herself a climax, but something held her back. She felt like her release…belonged to him.

From the first moment, she'd felt she was his. The way he watched her, how he seemed aware of her every movement when they were together in the lab, as if she was a part of him already, seemed only to underscore it.

That third night, she'd been staring into the microscope, mentioning some variables she'd researched during the day that he might find intriguing. She'd started as his hands molded over her hips, his body sliding against hers as he put his mouth on her neck. His large hand cruised up her thigh, the silk lining of her skirt brushing her flesh as he pushed beneath it and found her sex with capable fingers. The second he touched her, she started to vibrate, and he'd murmured against her ear.

"Now you can come. You've been waiting for me to tell you that you can, haven't you?"

"Yes," she gasped. She came in a matter of seconds, his mouth swallowing her cries as he took command of her lips, stroked her straining body. He cradled her jaw as the aftershocks rocked her, and she remembered jerking at his sharp nip at her throat, another bolt of pleasure spearing through her at the pain.

It wasn't the kind of memory one shared with one's grandfather. Though it was indelibly printed in her mind, it was only a quick flash through her head now.

Her grandfather touched her hand. "Is he a good man, Debra?"

"Yes. One of the best, Grandfather. Good like you, though I think he's still learning how to get there. We both are."

He nodded. "You don't see him through rose-colored glasses. That's good for both of you. Can't really love someone you set on a pedestal. Loving someone…it's about knowing them, and that's a lifelong puzzle. Biggest unsolved question there is. Like living a worthwhile life. I know you're on the right road. I see worries, but determination... A belief that you're where you're...meant to be."

His eyes were starting to droop, voice starting to slur. "You have to go tonight, don't you?"

"I can stay longer." She knew she could. Brian had said so.

Her grandfather shook his head, his eyes opening again with visible effort. "No need for you to be around for this part. This is between me and your grandmother. She has help to carry the load I've become. But I'm so glad to see your face once more. You think of your grandfather now and again, all right?"

She cried again then, silent tears. When she hugged him, she felt his thin arm against her back, his fingers so tentative in their brush against her shoulder blade. He'd had such a strong grip. Now she was the one with the strong grip. Holding him, she stroked his hair until he fell asleep. It happened in minutes, just as her grandmother had warned.

She finally made herself straighten. She traced the thin wisp of hair over his brow. Bent and kissed his hand, so limp on the covers. Then she rose, turning toward her grandmother. Vivian was a quiet, brittle statue in the corner. Debra crossed the room to her, held her tight as well, as long as her grandmother needed, a million unspoken words in the embrace.

Brian heard all the thoughts in her head, all the things she wanted to say, all the apologies. She knew this would be the last time she'd see them. She didn't let go until her grandmother stroked her hair, eased back.

"I love you," Debra said brokenly.

"And we love you, Debra. Always."

Debra nodded, squeezing her grandmother's hand lightly, mindful of her arthritis, though Brian could tell she wanted to hold onto her with all her strength. It was a major act of will for her to leave the room, come back up the hall to him, every footstep resounding in an aching heart.

She gave him a nod, letting him know it was time to go. He'd already risen, but she stayed along the wall, out of reach, moving toward the door. It was clear she felt too breakable to be touched.

At the door, she stopped, closed her eyes and inhaled. She wanted the scents of growing up to fill her, the things she'd learned here, never to be forgotten. Glancing around the quiet room, he sensed her grandmother in that back bedroom, waiting because she didn't have the strength to show her granddaughter to the door. Pushing down a wealth of inexplicable feeling, Brian followed Debra out, closing the door behind him.

She moved down the walkway quietly. He shook his head at the driver, opened the door for her himself, steadying her with a hand on her elbow. As he turned to get in the limo with her, he saw Vivian at the bedroom window. She didn't raise her hand in farewell, and Brian knew she was crying again. The ache inside his own chest was difficult to manage. Like Debra, he didn't really have words for what couldn't be changed, decisions that had been made. How could Debra not have regrets?

"He said she has help?"

"Yes."

He didn't have to give Debra access to his mind for her to understand the question before it was asked. "My aunt lives here, and my mother's emails say she and her family have been helping my grandmother care for him. She's not alone."

As Brian studied her profile, her chin lifted so she inadvertently revealed eyes brimming with tears in the reflection of the dark window, he wondered if his servant felt she could say the same.

He wanted to reach out, close his hand over hers, but she still had that invisible wall around her. He knew it would only take the right combination of words to crack it. So he used them.

"You know," he said, "Just because you made your choice, doesn't mean you don't have every right to grieve for the path not taken."

She turned her head. Tears streamed down her face. He couldn't bear it.

Come here.

He opened his arms and she went into them. He'd never held her when she cried like this. Though she didn't give in to tears often, he was sure she'd done so more than once since she'd made the choice to be his servant and turn away from all this. He knew for certain she'd cried the night he was so cruel to her.

From here forward, whenever you need to cry, I will hold you. For as long as you need it.

Just as she had her grandmother. Strong women didn't need to be held endlessly. Just at the right moment, to give them the strength to keep going.

Her body shuddered, and he held her tighter, afraid she might physically break apart from the storm of emotions he felt rushing through her. But she was still his Debra, his spirited, impossibly strong servant. When that storm ebbed, he heard her response.

Same goes, my lord.

He'd never known a smile could hurt.

Chapter Six

When they landed in Texas on Butch Dorn's private airstrip, there'd been little time for anything but a few pleasantries and being shown to the guest quarters before the vampires had to retire for the dawn. She was glad for that, because the attack of weeping had left her drained. She hadn't cried so hard and so long in…maybe ever. She'd found herself crying for her grandfather, for the life she'd left behind, for the night Brian had sex with the other woman…for everything. True to his word, Brian had held her through all of it, even when she was so overcome by her emotions she could barely breathe. He'd rubbed her back, soothed her, held her. Just held her.

She'd been given a small adjoining room to his, the usual set up for vampire and servant, so Brian could call her to him at his pleasure, but once they reached their guest quarters, Brian caught her hand. "You'll stay with me, at least for a few hours."

She wasn't really sure she could sleep. She had a tension headache from all the crying, and her third mark constitution wasn't making it go away.

"You just need a change of focus." Bringing her over to the bed, he sat down, moved her between his spread knees and began to undress her.

He unbuttoned and pushed her blouse off her shoulders, unhooked her bra, then removed her skirt and underwear while she held his shoulder. She could only study him numbly, bemused as he cosseted her. He'd unbalanced her with his kindness, his attentiveness. But he apparently knew she needed more than his kindness to let go of the pain that was making her temples throb.

He laid her on her back, his eyes sparks in the darkness because he hadn't turned on any lights. She had an impression of heavy, rustic furniture, appropriate and comfortable for a Texas setting. The room smelled faintly of sage and rosemary.

Brian stretched out next to her, stroking the hair at her temple, curling a long strand around his forefinger. He hadn't undressed, but her hand rested on the first closed button of his shirt, her fingertips sliding over the warm, firm flesh revealed in the open collar above it. She stared up at him in the darkness, no words to say, just okay to be this with him, in the semi-darkness. Then his hand closed over her wrist.

"You know the best way to get rid of a headache? Other than to stake the vampire causing it?"

She smiled. "That sounds like something Gideon would say."

"Well, a scientist has to steal humor from others, because it's widely known we have none of our own. Do you know the best way to get rid of a headache, Debra?"

"No my lord. Aspirin doesn't really work for third marks."

"No, it doesn't. But a refresher on basic anatomy should. Trust your doctor."

Her lips retained a faint curve. Though his main focus was research, Brian had done as much study for medical practice as possible. The daylight requirements of internship and residency had denied him the ability to complete the degree. However, he regularly treated injuries to the second marked staff at the Council quarters and his in-depth understanding of anatomy had been invaluable to his research. Vampire anatomy wasn't significantly different from human. It was the constitution itself that set the species apart.

She knew it chafed him that he didn't have the degree, though he already had several in other fields. At some point she was sure he'd figure a way around that daylight requirement. A vampire's longevity allowed for a great deal of education, if he was willing to pursue it. And he was.

"I appreciate my servant's faith in me."

He leaned over her, clasped her hand, kissed her knuckles. Cupping the side of her head, he nuzzled her ear, then behind and below it, placing his lips just...there.

"Oh..." A faint sigh escaped her lips as he caressed the highly erogenous zone. He'd released her hand and it rested on his chest again. She wished his shirt wasn't in the way.

Unbutton it, then.

She did, laying her hand fully on his solid chest. She averted her face, giving him better access. He was just playing in that small area behind her ear, but it was enough to make her body shift restlessly, hips pressing into the bed.

"So what part is this?" he said. "Until you remember, I can't move on to another part."

She managed a half laugh. "Mastoid process. Lowest...point of the temporal lobe."

"Hmm. No." He dropped a hand down between her legs, cupped her, pressed his fingers against her, making her moan. "Try again."

She fought through the haze of lust, realized the simple mistake. "Bone," she managed in a strangled voice. "Lowest point of the temporal bone."

"Correct. And this?" He moved to the side of her throat, his fangs grazing the muscle the turn of her head had made prominent, a long, slender cord.

"SCM."

"Full name." It was a gentle order, but he nipped her. Her headache did seem to be lessening, though she was fairly certain it wasn't the anatomy lesson doing the trick.

"Sternocleidomastoid muscle. Because it attaches sternum... clavicle... and mastoid process." She had to swallow another desperate chuckle as he followed her explanation, laying a moist kiss on her sternum, clavicle and back up beneath her ear again. "Brian..."

He stilled at her whisper, but then resumed, his kisses slower, longer, the pressure holding, such that she could feel the shell over her heart cracking, those openings growing wider, willing her to invite him in, grip that vital organ in his hand and know that it was all his, whatever he wanted to do to it. This was insane.

"No, it's not. What I've been allowing us to be these past few years; that was insane. When we could have...this." He nuzzled her clavicle again. "You're so delicate. So...breakable."

The note in his voice made her look up at him, touch his face. He lifted his head to study her. "If I'd lost you that night, with Gideon...I'm not sure if I could have looked at anything in life the same way, Debra."

"Don't. I can't...not after tonight. Not right now."

After a pregnant pause, he nodded, bent his head again. "We'll revisit that later, then." He dropped a kiss in the hollow of her throat. "Manubrium."

He smiled against her flesh. She slid her fingers through his hair, even as she tugged his shirt off one shoulder, cupped the broad, smooth expanse. She slid the knuckles of her other hand over the firm ridges of his stomach.

"Rectus abdominis," she whispered. He was kissing his way down her sternum, tiny brushes of tongue and lips, a quick suction that had her moving in sinuous response. He kept on his downward track, mouth on her upper abdomen. Lower. Then, just when she thought he'd keep going past her pubic mound to her damp core, he moved over to her hip bone and upper thigh.

What area am I covering, sweet servant? From ear to pubis…to legs…I don't intend to miss a single inch.

She was going to turn to flame, burn to ash right here. Her headache was gone. "Superficial front line. Connective tissue…from toes, front of legs to ASIS, the protrusion of pelvic bone…then from there to the pubic bone…"

She arched up as his mouth went back there, just above her clit. He traced the crescent of her mound, nipping at her with his lips, a fang.

"Spread your legs for me, Debra. Wide."

He spoke against her flesh, and when she complied, he settled himself between her legs, elbows on either side of her hips.

His mouth went back to her rectus abdominis, which was firm and flat. Servants as well as vampires pursued a rigorous schedule of hand-to-hand and weaponry training, for the world they inhabited could be dangerous, but even with that, her stomach didn't have the sectioned definition his did. It was ironic that female servants had to work twice as hard to build up the muscle layers the male servants did, with even more ease than their human counterpoints.

Because the gods know male vampires like their women softer to the touch.

He moved from there back up the three parts of the sternal bone—xiphoid process, sternal body, manubrium—God. She lifted her chin to let him lick and play with that sensitive hollow in her throat, then he was back over the SCM to the mastoid process again. That wonderfully sectioned stomach was firmly against her core, and she wanted to writhe, mark him with her wet folds.

"Sure you don't want to cover the reproductive system?" she breathed. He chuckled, a masculine caress against her ear.

"I plan to cover it." He bit her ear lobe. "Explore it, penetrate it. Fuck you into oblivion."

"Okay." She closed her eyes. *Thank you.* All of it was going away except him, and she didn't have the strength to be afraid of that.

He lifted her up to turn her on her stomach, and worked back down from the nape, the spine.

"Keep your legs spread wide."

She quivered at that, obeyed. When he reached her buttocks, he adjusted himself so his elbows were braced outside her thighs. He cupped her ass, thumbs spreading her cheeks, and put his mouth on her rim.

"God…" She was so sensitive there and he knew it. She fisted the sheets in both hands, looking for anything to anchor herself.

I'm your anchor. "Lift your hands above the bedding, palms flat, fingers open. No moving your hips." *Your Master wants you very, very still.*

It was impossible, her body making convulsive jerks as he licked and thrust his tongue inside her, strong hands holding her spread wide. She pleaded with him, she knew not for what, but she knew his intent was to completely exhaust her.

You mistake me, servant. My intent is to pleasure myself with your response.

A tart ripple went through her at the ruthless note to his mind voice. Lifting her up onto her knees, he put his mouth between her legs. And the orgasm hit her out of left field.

There was no warning, no time to ask, nothing, but she knew he'd planned it that way. She had no control of her body, so her hands were back on the bed, fingers clutching the covers as the climax rocked her, the petals of her sex slick against his mouth, the tissues spasming so she felt their movement against his firm lips. Turning her over with that vampire quickness, so her climax didn't experience even a hitch, he opened his slacks and sunk himself inside her, shoving her up to another pinnacle.

He was hard and thick, stretching her vibrating tissues, goading her aftershocks to higher levels. He withdrew enough to stroke through the wetness of her outer labia with the head of his cock, coy thrusts that had her moving against him still. He pushed back into her, held her on his loins, his gaze pinning her as he set an easy rhythm.

He was diabolical. Despite the fact she was just coming off one climax, she wanted to take that flight with him, again and again. His maddeningly even pacing drove her into an intense, emotional arousal, one that wrapped around her, held her in sensual paralysis. He bent his head, kissed and bit her throat, her sternum, curled his fingers in her hair and tugged. She arched and lifted her hips, taking him deeper, and felt arousal uncurl again.

He didn't alter his pace or patience until she shuddered to a second conclusion under the grip of his hands. She gazed up at him, wild-eyed, her fingernails digging into his back, his waist, his name on her lips.

"Please, Master. Come for me."

He gave her a nod, his gaze like the swirling gray-green clouds of an impending storm. His jaw tightened, then all those pleasing muscles shifted against her, hips flexing under her crossed calves.

"Yes…please," she pleaded.

He let himself go then, gentleness and patience gone. Levering up her hips with bruising hands on her buttocks, he thrust into her harder. She wished those bruises wouldn't heal so quickly, so she could see them in the light of day. She liked any mark he left on her.

I'd mark you head to toe if I could.

"You have," she whispered as he brought his full weight down on her, curved his arms around her head while she curved hers over his back, hooked her hands on his shoulders so she could press her face close to his throat, feel his heart beat and the crashing pulse.

Even when he came down from that crest, he kept holding her close. He adjusted to the side, turned her to him, holding her in place with one proprietary hand cupped over her ass, the other over the back of her neck. They fell asleep that way, his breath stirring her hair, teasing the shell of her ear, her hands clutching his biceps.

§

Sometime during that sleep, they adjusted, so when she woke, she found she was curled in the curve of his body, his genitals against her buttocks, his chest against her back. It was around eight in the morning, her internal clock warning her she needed to get up and begin to prepare. Brian was in that sleep that sunrise inflicted upon him, and didn't stir as she held onto his arm wrapped over her, using it to help her turn over and look at him.

It was a difficult shelter to leave, but she knew her responsibilities. Plus she needed the bracing reminder of her usual routine. Brian had been kind to let her sleep with him. That quiet lovemaking, the playful anatomy lesson, was a balm on her raw heart, but she couldn't afford to forget his indulgences and kindnesses were entirely on his own sufferance. He was the vampire, she was the servant. She couldn't get in the habit of expecting such treatment, no matter his stated intent to make things different.

Why not?

She silenced her sullen inner voice, the one that Brian's change in behavior had sparked. Brian had said he loved her. In the privacy of their shared minds, the physical moments they alone shared, that could all be well and good, but as good as it felt, she wasn't going to let herself get carried away with it. As she'd told Jacob, in the end, love didn't mean the same thing to vampires.

Though she had to admit, for the past few days, he'd not only lived up to her hopes, but surpassed them. In the end, that could be more dangerous to her than no change at all.

No. She couldn't think that way. It was only dangerous if she opened herself up too widely to possibilities that were likely futile.

Accept what is, expect nothing different. And definitely, always, live in the moment.

She touched his face. Eventually, he would reach an age where he wouldn't sleep as deeply once sunrise happened. There were pros and cons to that. Good, in that he could touch her mind later in the morning when questions cropped up and she wanted to bounce ideas off him. Bad, in that she couldn't have the opportunity to do this, simply touch him and know she was doing something only a full servant had the right and ability to do, watching over her Master as he slept.

Suppressing a sigh, she slid out of the bed, did a quick run through the shower, got dressed. Despite her gratitude for the extra sleep, she knew they needed to maximize their time here. She'd lost vital hours toward preparing for that. In addition to their research needs, she also had to address the things all servants coordinated for their Master or Mistress in a guest household. She needed to introduce herself one-on-one to Butch's servant, Dix Conner, and visit the rest of the household staff to determine the set up for caring for her Master's needs. That included finding out the daily schedule, to ensure they were courteous guests.

Like most vampires, Brian assumed his servant would handle such matters, though fortunately he was far less demanding in that regard. Most of his needs in any new environment related to his working conditions, which meshed with her own requirements, since her primary role was working alongside of him.

Part one of her plan, introducing herself to Butch's servant, would have to wait. The housekeeper told her Dix was out in the pastures with the other hands, moving cattle. Definitely a far cry from servant responsibilities at the Council estate, though Jacob did pitch in on home maintenance and landscaping at times, because he had skills in that area and enjoyed exercising them.

The only other high level servant she knew who was employed in that type of labor was Dev, Debra's second favorite servant in the whole world. His Mistress, Lady Daniela, lived in Western Australia, on a sheep farm with thousands of acres. Dev was often gone during the day or out working on the compound. When Brian and Debra had visited them there, Dev had taken her to see the sheep one morning, let her witness a shearing. He'd twirled a sheep on her hips like she was dancing with him. Dev divested her of her coat so quickly it was no more than a trip to the barber shop to the animal, sent back out to pasture with a new, cooler haircut.

Since Dix wasn't available, she went in search of the housekeeper. Yolanda, a quiet Mexican woman with expressive dark eyes and a mouth set in a straight line, was also the cook, so she provided Debra the necessary information about dinner plans. "We're expecting six of them tonight, including Lord Brian and Butch. We'll set up in the main dining room."

Four vampires other than Butch and Brian. Not a large number, not by Council standards. It should have quelled the tension in her stomach, but she hadn't yet heard the guest list. Maybe the one she feared wasn't on it. A vampire didn't reach overlord status without being a force to be reckoned with, but Butch didn't seem overly hung up on formality. When Brian had introduced her last night and she'd bowed with a respectful "my lord", the gray-eyed vampire who looked like he could wrestle bulls to the ground had chuckled.

"Just call me Butch, miss. Lord Butch just doesn't have the right ring to it. And while my given name Caleb works well enough, barely anyone calls me that, so I wouldn't even know to be listening for it."

"Who will be in attendance?" She tried to sound casual, but when Yolanda glanced down, Debra realized she'd clenched the fingers of her right hand into a ball.

"Just three vampires from his territory, senorita. Plus Lord Graham, the California overlord."

Her nails cut into her palm, drawing blood. "Thank you," she said.

Yolanda gave her a quizzical look, but Debra nodded and withdrew. As she moved back through the halls toward the study Butch had given them to set up for their work, she realized her shoulders were tense as a board and she was hesitating at corners or when passing closed doors. It was broad daylight. Damn it, she should be past this rabbit-like behavior when it came to Lord Graham. Or any vampire.

Vampires were always unpredictable. Any sensible servant eschewed overfamiliar behavior with them, even if they seemed eminently approachable, like Butch Dorn. But she admitted she'd liked him on sight, whereas she'd been repulsed by Lord Graham from the first time they'd met.

It had been at her first Vampire Gathering. He'd latched onto her inexperience, her discomfort with all of it. Brian's status then had been far less, and Graham was significantly older, around four hundred fifty. Strength grew with a vampire's age, and might equaled right in the vampire world. A visiting vampire with seniority and greater strength could avail himself of the servant of a lower ranking vampire. However, most vampires observed an unspoken courtesy, only enjoying the pleasures of that servant where the servant stayed in view of, and essentially under the command, of the Master or Mistress. The exception at Gatherings were the lowest echelon servants who were recruited to be valets, wait staff and domestics for the duration of the event. Fortunately, Debra had avoided that. Mostly.

Lord Graham had cornered her in a hallway of the estate where the Gathering was held. He'd stopped her with a casual wave, his gaze sweeping over her.

"A pretty young thing. Lord Brian's servant. New to all this, aren't you? Your first Gathering?"

"Yes, my lord."

When he reached out toward her, she'd jumped, unable to help herself. He'd chuckled. "A little nervous. Nervousness implies resistance, and your job isn't to resist, is it?"

He'd waited patiently for her dutiful "No, my lord." Then he'd drawn her to him. She'd been holding an armful of files from the Council archives she'd intended to scan to digital media, but he had her set those on the floor. Then he pulled open her blouse with as much subtlety as a punch in the face. Most vampires enjoyed arousing a servant, which initially had been one of the hardest things for her to handle at these events, since she'd felt she was betraying her loyalty to Brian. She didn't have that worry with Lord Graham. Her skin crawled at his touch.

Tearing the front joining point of her bra, careless of the expense of the garment, he'd fondled and squeezed her breasts as if considering the selections of a fruit bowl. She'd stiffened, almost drawing away, but she'd stopped herself. Not quickly enough. He'd noticed.

Graham was her first experience with a vampire with an overdeveloped sadistic streak. He enjoyed "initiating" new servants, exploiting their inexperience like a Viking raider taking a virgin. Since Debra had never been able to find a consistent level of comfort with such things, every time they met, it was like she was new candy to him once more.

That horrible day, he'd stood in the hall, making her stay still as he pinched her nipples to hardness, kept playing with them. During a Gathering, the meeting locale was filled to overflowing with other servants and vampires, so the eyes of passersby were upon her. Several vampires stopped to talk with him. She was revolted, but averted her gaze to the open space past his shoulder. Enduring.

"None of that." He pinched her roughly enough to earn a gasp, her eyes snapping back to him. "You keep your entire focus on the vampire you're serving, girl. While keeping your gaze at my feet." He leaned in, his breath on her ear. "I can tell when you're paying attention."

He'd had her pick up the files a few minutes later, but he hadn't dismissed her as she'd hoped. He'd taken her off to a side hall, out of the flow of foot traffic. It quickly became obvious he removed them to the quieter spot for his own concentration, not to spare her any humiliation. Pushing her to her knees, he made her keep the files on her thighs, her hands locked on them like a form of restraints. Then he shoved his cock in her mouth and made her service it until he jetted. When he did, he pulled out, spilled himself on her face and her breasts, splattering the files.

Zipping up, he patted her on the head like a cocker spaniel and nodded. "I'll look forward to seeing you again." He said it almost kindly, but she saw the avarice in his eyes. "You're a sweet morsel."

She'd struggled to her feet after he left, mopped her face with her torn blouse, then gone back to the wing of the lab where Brian wasn't. She'd thrown up a couple times, scrubbed off with topical until she gave herself a rash, and scanned the files into the database before she threw the copies away.

Up until that time, she and Brian had spent so much time traveling, she hadn't had to experience many interactions with other vampires, and certainly nothing like that. As a result, she lived in terror of a future encounter, and especially of the next Gathering. Fortunately, Graham wasn't in attendance at the next one. But Lady Lyssa and Jacob were.

It was her second meet with Jacob at a formal event. Largely because of his efforts and Dev's, she started to realize the public sexual requirements of servants could be pleasurable, with the right perspective and focus. Though she always had that flush of nerve-wracking panic where she thought "I can't do this", she got through. The negative feelings only returned at the end when, her heart rate still racing from her climax, her body vibrating, she watched other servants return to the sides of their aroused Master or Mistress to reap the rewards of serving their desires so well. All while hers was off in his lab, assuming she was taking care of her servant duties in a way that reflected well upon him.

She'd learned to deal with that sense of emptiness that came at the end of a climax where he wasn't watching, listening, participating. Yet it was so much easier when he was there. It was actually genuine then, how aroused she became with his eyes on her, his commands in her mind. Everything she did, or was done to her, was at his pleasure.

Him being present or not, her service at a public event was part of being a servant. A part she thought she handled passably well now, except for Graham. Fortunately, she only had to interact with Graham on rare occasions. But when those occasions happened, she knew it was going to be terribly unpleasant when he caught her alone. Not if. He made sure of that.

She guessed she should count herself lucky he'd never tried to fuck her. That wasn't to spare her, though. If the vampire master in question wasn't involved in the decision, even a lower-ranking one like Brian, it crossed the official lines of etiquette.

If Graham had ever made that demand and Brian agreed, she thought that would have been the end for her, her soul simply collapsing in on itself.

It could still happen though, couldn't it? Tonight, even.

Stop it, she told herself. *Stop borrowing trouble.*

For one thing, Graham had never done any of it in Brian's presence. With that hateful vampire intuition, he'd obviously figured out she coped better with Brian close.

But though Butch's place was a nice-sized estate, it wasn't the maze of hallways of the Council compound or a Gathering locale. She tamped down the tight ball of apprehension in her stomach. If she could stay with Brian throughout the evening, then Graham shouldn't succeed in getting her alone.

She could tell herself Graham was no different from any other vampire, but he gave her a sense of dread and fear she couldn't hide, and he exploited it. He was a sexual predator.

Given that vampires were the top predator in the food chain and their servants were essentially sex slaves when they wanted to exercise their libidinous nature, it sounded laughable, but she knew she was right. Most other servants were experienced enough to please him without setting off his sadism trigger, but in those breakfast discussions, it was clear he was no one's favorite. No one else seemed to fear him as she did, though. She wished she had their fortitude.

She set her jaw. She did, damn it. She was an accomplished scientist as well as a dedicated vampire's servant, and damn good at both jobs. She'd had a few weak instances these past couple of days, and her Master had indulged them, but it was time to prove herself worthy of that consideration, the way Jacob did with his Mistress. He didn't whine and moan about this kind of thing.

Arriving in Butch's spacious study, her gaze swept the room. It was decorated in western colors and masculine appointments, like the vast main desk, long sofa and five large flat screens where he could mix and match simultaneous viewing options. She'd requested a couple folding tables and they were already here.

Pushing aside her worries about the evening, she got down to work. It didn't take too long to lay out everything, but once she opened up her laptop and Brian's side by side, there was email to check and reports to download from the Alabama and Berlin facilities, as well as from the teams they had out in the field. Answering questions via video chat, compiling data, studying results and making her notes kept her busy for quite some time.

As a result, when the sound of a cleared throat at the study door had her lifting her head and looking around, she was surprised to realize it was mid-afternoon.

Dix Conner was standing in the doorway. The rangy, sunbaked man looked every inch a true cowboy in his dusty boots and jeans, a holstered knife at his belt and a pair of battered work gloves tucked in his waistband. His open-necked cotton shirt was stained with sweat and clung to his tough body. He smelled not unpleasantly of grass, horses and cows.

She'd had a brief look at him last night, but here it was evident what a good match he was with Butch. Butch Dorn was tall and magnetic, a broad-shouldered big man with piercing gray eyes and a thick silk mane of dark hair, saved from prettiness by his rugged features. Though a human lost most scars when turned to a vampire, she'd noted a unique trait to Butch. Though his skin hadn't seen sun in almost three centuries, he was nearly as tanned as Dix. It was as if the sun had been stamped on him, as much a part of him as blood and bone. The Texas outdoor life suited both of them, even if Butch only experienced it at night.

"Yolanda said you might need some food," Dix said.

He was carrying a couple thick sandwiches and what appeared to be homemade potato chips, still warm and fragrant from the oven. "Figured I'd come share lunch with you and find out what you're going to do to the big lab rat tonight. Butch also wanted me to go over any info I can give you up front before we have to deal with that pointless waste of time known as dinner."

"That's very kind." She gave him an appreciative smile. "I am sorry about that. Honestly, I think Brian would have been just as happy to focus on his work and have takeout."

"Amen to that. But don't worry. I wasn't pinning this on Lord Brian." Dix waved a hand and pulled up a chair on the other side of the small table so they could both eat. "Butch knows some things you have to do when it comes to vampires, just to remind everyone of their place in the scheme of things. Vampires who get too informal and unstructured tend to start walking outside the lines. Hope I didn't offend."

"You couldn't possibly," she said, and he grinned at her graciousness, pushing a few more chips her way.

"Eat up. There are plenty more in the kitchen, even more than the other hands can eat, if that's possible. Yolanda must have imported all the potatoes in Ireland. You know we won't get to eat until late tonight. But I always prefer to eat two or three hours before these things, make sure digestion isn't an issue, if you get my drift."

For a few blissful hours, she'd forgotten about dinner. Now her stomach curdled. She took only one more bite of sandwich before giving up and taking a drink of the sweet tea instead.

"Something the matter?" Dix asked, concern creasing his weathered brow. His brown hair was spiky and short and she noticed an old scar near the hair line. Third marks didn't always lose their scars, either. Nor their inhibitions from their former life, unfortunately.

She straightened. "No. Not at all. Are the other vampires already here?"

"Yeah. Most arrived last night. Texas is a pretty big area, so they tend to come a day early to avoid sun exposure. You guys were the last to arrive." Dix watched her closely, eyes shrewd in a way that reminded her of Jacob.

"It'll be okay," he said. "Butch doesn't let things get too out of hand. You've done this before, right?"

"Yes, of course. Really, it's fine." She grimaced, looked down at the plate. "It's nothing. I've had some unpleasant dealings with Lord Graham, but nothing that we don't expect, right?"

"Yeah, that one's an asshole."

Her gaze snapped up at his bald statement. "I think Butch was hoping he'd have better things to do tonight," Dix continued, "but since his and Butch's territories are adjacent, and Graham's always angling for Region Master—God help us if and when that happens—Graham's not going to miss an opportunity to show up and prove he has the biggest dick in the room. Shame he doesn't realize there's a difference between having one and being one."

She choked on a laugh and the sweet tea. Dix helpfully patted her back, giving her an encouraging smile as she regained composure. Bless the generous hearts of servants. Some of them could be as much a cross to bear as their Master or Mistress, but she'd had far more experience with those like Jacob and Dix.

She could do this. She'd just stay close to Brian. And whatever happened at the dinner, Brian would be there. Even Brian wouldn't beg off of a dinner this small, especially since he was the unofficial guest of honor.

"All right, then." She wiped her mouth with a napkin and took up her tablet. "Let's see what questions we can get done."

§

Dinner was scheduled for 11pm to give Brian time to do what he needed. Butch submitted to the physical and tissue and blood sampling without complaint. When Debra drew the blood, finding a vein wasn't a problem. The bulge of muscles along his arms were vein-rich.

"So any vampires have an irrational fear of needles?" Butch asked, his breath stirring the hair of her bent head.

"I'm sworn to secrecy on that," she said.

"We'll see. I don't know a woman alive who can't be bribed by Yolanda's chocolate empanadas." Butch lifted his attention to Brian. "So explain to me again why you think I'm the ideal guinea pig for your study?"

Brian glanced at his monitor, tapped a few keys. "Because you're one of the most stable made vampires, according to your age and history," he said absently. "If we can understand the factors that contributed to that, we can make better decisions on which willing humans to turn to increase our own species. All while simultaneously working on increasing fertility rates of the born vampires."

"Mongrels are usually the healthiest dogs," Dix noted. He was sitting on a nearby stool, rotating back and forth with the help of one booted foot.

Butch gave him a wry look. "With the exception of scrappy strays like you."

"I wasn't the one letting a little sun keep me from doing a hard day's work. The cows were in a hell of a mood today. Like herding a bunch of cats. Think it must be a full moon."

"If I threaten to disembowel him in front of you, is that a sign of instability?" Butch queried. Reaching out with his free hand, he touched the corner of Debra's mouth. "See, I made her smile. Told you I could do it, Dix."

Her gaze lifted, but Brian was standing just behind Butch, so it was his eyes that drew her. He was studying her with an unreadable look. Then he turned back to his laptop. The machine was set up on his portable desk which could be telescoped so he could use it while standing, like now.

"Can you tell me about the fertility results?" Butch asked. "Lady Annette showed us overlords the report, but would be nice to hear it from the horse's mouth. The scuttlebutt is that vampires and servants who are too friendly with one another are far more likely to conceive."

The official public report had removed "deep romantic love" and replaced it with "closer relationships". The Council wasn't ready to throw the other term out there. However accurate, they felt it was too much of a paradigm change, too soon.

"So if I care too much for Dix, I could get him knocked up?" Butch ventured.

She tried to smother the chuckle. Butch grinned at her. "You better leave her here, Brian. She's awful pretty when she laughs."

"Born vampires have been known to have occasional surges of disembowelment-inducing instability," Brian noted. "You might remember that."

His tone was dry, and he didn't take his eyes from his screen as he spoke. But Debra looked his way anyhow. He wasn't usually possessive, even in a teasing vein.

He lifted his gaze, met hers. This time his expression was far more readable, causing a pleasant flutter in her chest.

Butch snorted. "You still didn't answer my question about Dix."

"Get him pregnant, we'll be opening a whole other research wing," Brian returned. "And you'll need someone else to move your cows around. Restrain your fondness for him, because I expect it's far more difficult to find a good foreman than to get him pregnant. Now, back to the questions…"

The night she'd left with Gideon and Anwyn, she'd told Brian if the worst happened, he'd merely need to find a new lab assistant. She remembered the way he'd looked at her, what he'd said.

"You think that is all your value to me?"

"I never assume my worth is greater than what it is."

He was making it impossible for her to adhere to all the things he'd taught her about vampire-servant relationships.

Sometimes what we know and believe needs to change.

She stilled at the sensual murmur in her mind. She could feel his attention on her again, but this time she kept hers on her task, watching the overlord's blood fill the vials. At the dinner tonight, she was going to need all her shields in place. She couldn't afford to make herself too vulnerable. So she lifted a shoulder, an acknowledgment but not an answer, and focused on the work, the one thing that could never confuse her enough to risk her soul.

§

It took a couple more hours for Brian to get what he needed. Dix didn't stay for the whole thing, coming and going to check in with the housekeeper on matters Butch wanted verified for the dinner, but during the times he was there, it was clear there was an exceptional rapport between the two men.

Gathering extra data for other qualifying projects like the fertility study and vampire-servant relationships took more time than they'd scheduled, but it was worth it to corroborate what they had so far. Though the personal value of a servant was an issue most vampires didn't feel comfortable discussing, Debra had helped him develop the questions that produced indicators the vampire wouldn't directly supply. This time, such obfuscations weren't necessary. Butch cut through the subtle phrasing after no more than two questions.

"You want to know how I feel about him," the Texas overlord said. He had an amused gleam in his eye. "Don't look surprised. We all know you born folk don't expect any better behavior out of us made rabble. Ironically that means I can be more honest about it than you, no offense intended. Dix has saved my ass more times than I can count these past decades. He's the best part of my day and night, and I'd rip the heart out of anyone who tried to take him from me. Yeah, we're vampire and servant and I love wrestling him down to his hands and knees and teaching him who's boss, but we're a team. That clear enough for your survey?"

"Crystal," Brian said. "Given the conclusions we reached from the fertility study, it's actually a shame he isn't female."

"Not from my perspective," Butch said. "I love a woman's cunt and pretty, high-sitting tits like your lab assistant here has, but faced with the choice between them and a man's tight ass, I'll go for him every time. Just how I'm wired."

Debra was staring at the Texas overlord, but when Brian glanced toward her, she ducked her head, tapping on her tablet again. He suppressed his frustration. She'd been nigh inaccessible to him this evening, and he wasn't sure why she was so determined to focus on nothing but the work, not allowing her thoughts to stray left or right from it.

He'd have tried a deeper probe of her mind, but they were on a timetable. The visiting vampires from Butch's territory had passed outside the study several times throughout the early evening, but they hadn't stepped in to speak to him. Butch had explained he'd told them Brian was doing important research, and they weren't to be interrupted.

"Otherwise we'd never finish before dinner." The overlord winked. "I've taken pains to invite three of my more interesting and less stuffy territory vampires, so it should be more relaxed than a Council event. My chef is also better."

Brian chuckled politely at that, half his mind caught up in the data Butch had provided them and how it meshed with the ongoing studies. Despite Butch's relationship with his servant being far more casual than the norm for an overlord, it appeared to have no negative impact on his effectiveness. Clearly comfortable with leadership and command, the man reeked alpha and Dominance in the same breath.

The two traits weren't always interchangeable. Brian knew he himself was undeniably a Dominant, but not necessarily an alpha. As a researcher, he was more concerned about the pursuit of knowledge, and had no difficulty deferring to Lyssa and the Council for other matters, though he could aggressively assert his viewpoint when necessary.

Mule-headed was what Lord Uthe called it, last time you argued a point with him.

He'd opened the conscious level of his mind to Debra to trade data points. She was obviously pleased enough with that connection to allow for some humor, but he still felt that tight reserve inside her. It hadn't pleased *him* that she'd been gone when he woke, but she couldn't be in two places at once, and their work was important to her, too. He couldn't be an ass, adding to her stress by making her to stay with him while she had tasks pending. Even if he had noticed the nightmares disappeared when he went to sleep with her next to him.

Lab assistant, Butch had called her. The overlords and Region Masters they met often referred to her that way. Even the Council members. At the Savannah facility, they had second marked, actual lab assistants, techs who did vital support work. But there was a distinct difference in education and status between a lab assistant and

Debra. She operated the entire research facility in Savannah during daylight hours, doing analysis, review and making testing decisions, just as he did during the night.

She was his partner, a researcher on an equal level with himself. God knows, he wouldn't have been able to tolerate anyone working with him who wasn't able to keep up, and she did more than that. She had areas where she surpassed him, seeing things intuitively that he came to by logic. It made them a very good team. Just as Butch said, right?

"With respect, my lord," he spoke abruptly. "I have to correct you. Debra is my servant, but she isn't my lab assistant. She holds two doctorates and quite frankly has areas where she can kick my brain's ass."

Butch glanced his way, the shrewd gray eyes studying him. He gave a nod, his lips twisting. "My opinion of you just went up a few notches, Lord Brian."

As for Debra, she'd come to a complete standstill. Brian suspected only his servant's normal tightly wound state was keeping her jaw from dropping. Since she was standing between Butch's knees, taking his vitals, listening to his heart and lungs, Butch picked up the stethoscope and tapped lightly, making her start. "*Doctor* Debra, then. My apologies, doctor."

Brian suppressed his irritation as Debra recovered enough to give the overlord a gently admonishing look, but there was a faint smile on her face, her cheeks flushed. Butch had re-settled his hands on her hips. Women responded to that personality type, didn't they? Handsome, charismatic and intensely attentive, a male like Butch could make a woman feel like the center of the universe, even a vampire's servant.

Dix returned then, reporting on some sundry ranch issue to Butch. It gave Brian some breathing room from his inexplicable jealousy to pay closer attention to what was happening. Though he might be having difficulty picking up anything from Debra's mind, Butch's attempts to get her to smile and relax seemed more purposeful than flirtatious, even more noticeable when Dix behaved in a similar manner toward her. He also noticed Dix watching Debra closely, with concern.

Damn it, why was he watching another vampire-servant pairing to figure out what was going on with his own? He was done skulking around the edges. No matter if it skewed the data or delayed dinner, he dove beneath that wall around her thoughts. He was going to find out what was going on, direct from the source.

It didn't take long for the effort to bear fruit. Butch had risen from the chair since the data collection done, and was shrugging into his shirt. Dix told Debra he'd see her at dinner, giving her hand a squeeze.

Her mind pinged like a submarine target.

Dinner. She was dreading dinner. And not the dread that came with enduring a social nicety. This was like she anticipated facing a firing squad.

Brian's brow furrowed as quiet descended on the library and she moved over to her laptop to finish her own computations. For a woman who didn't expect him to be in her mind, she kept things strapped down at a surprisingly cavernous level of her consciousness. But he'd just pointed it out to Butch, hadn't he? This wasn't an average woman's brain. Her brain was a tool she exercised and honed incessantly. She could likely manipulate data in her mind, classify and file it as securely as she could on a laptop.

He could push past all that, but she'd panicked when he'd gone there the other night, under far more sensual circumstances. She was already feeling very unsettled. He didn't want to add to it if he could figure it out through patience and deductive reasoning.

As the day had progressed, she had gotten quieter, less likely to respond to Butch's laughter. Once, when she needed to go to her room to retrieve a hardcopy file, Dix had hopped up and told her to tell him where it was. "That way you don't have to interrupt what you're doing," he'd said easily.

In hindsight, Brian realized he'd made the offer a little too quickly. But as a result, Debra had remained in the room with them throughout the day, never leaving except for the occasional bathroom break, which was just outside this room, in view of the door.

She regularly served at Council dinners. At the few where he'd also been present, he'd been incredibly pleased by her responsiveness. It was a credit to him as her Master and, beyond that, it intensely aroused him, feeling his servant act under his command. Up until recently, he'd always told himself it was evidence she'd positively adjusted to the realities of vampire life. But had he ever really delved into those subconscious layers where she was obviously hiding her true self, to see if emotionally she accepted the things a submissive like her responded to physically?

He knew she liked it very much when he was present at those events. Her eyes would latch onto him, mind reaching for him, ensuring her Master's pleasure. He hadn't seen it as a vital way for her to deal with the scenario. Endure it and find pleasure at the same time.

He frowned, prowling around her mind. She was focusing on her work, pushing her dread away, though he noticed the twitch of her fingers on the counter, the taut line of her shoulders. She was wearing her lab coat, as she always did when they were conducting official examinations, but beneath her slim body was clad in a waist-nipping skirt and cotton knit shirt that molded her curves. She'd change into something else for dinner, something a little more formal. Seeing the flash of it in her head, he was more than pleased with her choice.

She'd brought an amber-colored shimmery short dress, one of his favorites on her, enhancing her doe-brown eyes, the multiple shades of gold in her hair. His beautiful wild creature, something that looked like she belonged to the forest and in the shade of green trees. Even more pleasing was what she usually wore beneath it, thong panties and a matching bra whose cups were so low her generous breasts would spill out of them with little more than a shallow breath.

He just wasn't sure he cared to see the effect it would have on the other vampires present.

So you'd have her wear flannel? He couldn't afford to get possessive like this. He didn't have the rank to keep his servant exclusive. Truth, it had never occurred to him as a possibility. From the time he'd had a blood nanny, his parents had taught him a servant was a toy that must be shared, unless he achieved a rank where he could be more discriminating. A servant could only be kept completely to oneself if no vampire was higher in rank. There was only one position in the vampire world that qualified, and he didn't imagine himself taking Lyssa's place anytime soon.

His mind rejected the thought of Debra as a toy, though he knew the term simply clarified the example. He was being overly emotional. He returned to the matter at hand—figuring out the source of her fear in a way that didn't exacerbate it. "So, are you looking forward to dinner?"

"Yes, my lord."

Her response was automatic, but what happened in her mind was anything but. A maelstrom of thoughts and worries erupted with one face in the center of it. Lord Graham.

Another handful of images popped up around that center, and they had him coming to a full stop, his work forgotten. Any reservations about bonding himself too closely to her emotions vanished and he opened himself fully to the throbbing press of her fears, her dread. Fury filled him.

Over the past few days, he'd finally absorbed just how much Debra did for him. She not only cared for his needs as a vampire, which were demanding enough on their own, but she worked with him as well, a punishing schedule that had worked her to the bone. Past a third mark's endurance, until he noticed she wasn't getting any sleep.

She sure as hell hadn't planned to tell him.

Yes, he didn't have the rank to prohibit other vampires from enjoying the sensual pleasures his servant could offer, short of actual sex with her. Yet vampires who consented to other vampires taking liberties with their servants would at least stay in the servant's mind, even if just to enjoy voyeuristic pleasure. They didn't abandon their servant, mentally as well as physically, to face another vampire's requirements alone.

Debra's surprise when he'd issued the mild threat to Lord Butch about disembowelment underscored how rarely he demonstrated any possessiveness toward her at all. Many vampires did, which told others that those liberties, when taken, should be respectful of the vampire master or mistress. That there were consequences for stepping over the lines.

Unfortunately, he'd sent the exact opposite message. Then again, he'd never realized she'd faced such things. But that was because he didn't spend time in her mind. God in heaven, what kind of horrible bastard was he?

His lips tightened. The kind that would seize that cruel edge to use it for good purpose. For once.

He closed her laptop in mid-stream, though he allowed her time to remove her fingers from the keyboard first. Startled, she looked up at his face, which he knew was thundercloud dark.

"What else has Lord Graham made you do?"

Color stained her cheeks. That and the tremor that ran through her, her gaze dropping to the floor, were all the trademarks of a woman who felt shame. It only increased his wrath with himself.

"I'm sorry, my lord. I didn't want—"

"That's quite clear," he snapped. With effort, he reined himself back. "You owe me no apologies, Debra. Absolutely none."

Confusion gripped her. She was struggling for words, a question.

"You will tell me the things he has done," he said evenly. He'd seen snippets only. Probably more than enough to fill in the blanks, but he was going to be thorough. Unless it distressed her too much.

"I can't, my lord. Please don't make me say them."

He captured her chin in gentle fingers, met her eyes. "Show me then."

She did, staccato flashes as if she was trying to press the Play button but hit stop after each frame so she didn't have to see the animation. His blood boiled at what she revealed. No there hadn't been sex, but that hardly mattered, did it? Rape wasn't about sex.

His father would scoff at that. Brian could almost hear him, an obscene narrative to accompany what Debra was showing him. "A servant can't be raped. She's performed the same acts at public dinners, with other servants. Serving our pleasures is required of her."

It wasn't the same. There was a tremendous gap between those events, where her submissive nature allowed her to feel pleasure even if she had mental inhibitions—especially if he made the effort to make sure his ass was there to command her as her Master—and what Lord Graham had forced upon her.

He was still holding her chin, and he slid his grip briefly over her throat, gave it a light squeeze. "Debra."

"It's fine, my lord," she said hastily. "It's simply what a servant must do. I can handle it. It's fine. No need to trouble yourself. Will you be there tonight? I know there are things Butch gave us that you wish to review…"

She was trying her best to phrase it as a casual inquiry, but Brian saw the truth of it in her head, in her tremor beneath his touch. She wanted him there. Needed him there.

She'd never asked him for anything, not since the night she'd asked if he loved her. Every fiber of her was begging him to be there tonight, to help her through this. And what speared his heart was seeing how it shamed her to have to ask, to depend on him to care for her.

That answered his earlier question—yes, he was definitely a bastard. But he could change that.

It had been his experience that change didn't come about from external factors, only internal motivations. But Debra was his third mark, and that mark went both ways. She could delve down to the level of his soul, fill him to the brim, if he allowed it. Or even if he'd done his best to prevent it.

"Yes. I will be."

Her relief was palpable, but she merely nodded. Slipping out of his grasp, she gathered up her things as he watched her with narrowed eyes. "I'll go prepare for dinner," she said. "Is there anything else you require in the meantime?"

There were so many things, he couldn't enumerate them all. He was simmering with anger, frustration, regret...shame. He needed time to process things. As a result, though he was reluctant to leave it this way, he let her go.

"No, Debra. Go get ready for dinner."

She nodded, not meeting his eyes, and hurried out. He followed her in his mind to their room, noting how she hesitated at intersecting passageways. She was like a mouse scurrying through the estate, making sure the cat wasn't waiting to pounce.

He let the rage and helplessness in his heart rise. She'd pulled away from him so abruptly because she was afraid of depending on him too much. She was worried if she relied on him this one time, it would be harder for her to face it alone next time, since she was sure she would be.

Since the nightmares had started, he'd waffled between his upbringing, his risk to his career goals and his genuine feelings for his servant, but all he'd needed to do all along was step deeply enough inside her heart to unlock his own and face the stark truth.

He loved her.

He had made a major mistake, and what's worse, had kept making it, over and over again during their time together. He'd had his head buried in the sand ever since the night he'd "proven" to her what their relationship couldn't be. He'd had a few nightmares in his sleep? She'd been fucking forced to endure them in her waking hours.

Throughout his life, he'd experienced frustration over his rank and age. Over the scorn he received when he tried to get higher-ranking vampires to fund his work, validate it. Then there were all the years his father had been disappointed because Brian hadn't wanted to play political games, become a powerful overlord or Region Master. Even now, he was more pleased with Brian's rise in status than the strides toward keeping their species from extinction. No matter that an extinct species had no status to speak of.

All those frustrations dimmed next to this. It was the first time in his life he'd felt that stifled fury, not just for things close to his heart, but for someone inside it. Someone he should have been protecting all along.

He'd been so worried about proving he was a mature male, capable of making his own decisions. It was time to prove he *was* a man, in the only way that mattered. Following what his heart, mind and soul knew was right, not what others believed was right. No matter the cost, for Debra had already paid far more than he ever could.

Shutting down his computer, he resolved it was time to change for dinner—in more ways than one.

Chapter Seven

Debra was finishing her preparations when her Master spoke in her mind. *Don't leave the room without me. You'll accompany me to the dining room.*

It made her feel guilty. Because she'd revealed her worry about Lord Graham, now Brian felt the burden of protecting her. She'd tried to never be an obligation to him—

Are you trying to get me to punish you?

His sharpness brought her up short, left her confused. Was he angry about it, or about her thoughts? He was silent though, waiting for her response.

No, my lord. Unless that's what you desire. I apologize.

Nothing further, leaving her bemused. But when he sent her another thought a few minutes later, letting her know he was ready and she should meet him in the hall, she gave herself one last check and stepped out.

No sweater vest, no trace of the professor tonight. He wore a silver-gray dress shirt open at the throat, charcoal slacks and coat over it, polished Italian loafers. But clothing wasn't the only thing upgraded tonight. She was used to his absent-minded personality, as if his brain never completely left his work. She liked that about him. Yet she found this side of him appealing as well, if a little intimidating.

The sharp and cool hazel eyes that swept her showed a mind fully present in the here and now. His bearing suggesting a vampire who would take a leadership role in whatever situation presented itself to him. Strikingly, it reminded her of his father. And made her knees weaken in a way his father never had.

She was glad she'd taken extra effort tonight, though it had been motivated by an odd sort of defiance. She wasn't going to fear the Lord Grahams of the world. She was going to dress for her Master's pleasure.

You succeeded.

She warmed at his praise, even as the lock of his gaze, potent as a steel cuff, gave her an additional quiver. She'd brought the amber dress because she knew he liked it. Though she didn't wear it often, it made the most of her slim figure, the breast-hugging bra beneath lifting her generous breasts and providing ample cleavage. The short skirt revealed her legs to the thigh. The sprinkle of sparkles made her feel dressed up. She'd worn her hair down, brushing it into waves around her face, even applying extra makeup to enhance the set of her eyes, make her lips glisten.

He studied her from head to toe, his eyes resting briefly on the three-inch black pumps she'd chosen, hoping she wouldn't trip and break a limb. But she wasn't going to be the nervous ingénue tonight. If she could finally pull off the attitude of an experienced servant, unfazed by anything thrown at her at a vampire dinner, Lord Graham's sadistic urges would be left unsatisfied and he would lose interest in her going forward. Brian's concern had been a wakeup call. She was a capable, strong woman, and she could handle this. She would be a credit to him, not an encumbrance.

His protracted appraisal was helping her confidence considerably. His gaze slid back up her legs, over the curve of hip, then lingered a long time on her breasts. When his attention shifted to her throat, she felt her pulse jump. His look was intense, heated, full of things she couldn't completely comprehend.

When she shifted, he lifted a finger, a nonverbal command to stay still. He circled her, reaching out to mold a hand over her waist, cup her buttock. He was a solid strong male wall at her back as he dropped a kiss on her collar bone. His other hand came up, took a possessive hold of her breast. Touching what belonged to him in a way that provoked a soft moan from her, all her nerves reacting.

She'd worn shimmery stockings attached with garters, tiny bows at the clasps. He traced the strap of one, hooking beneath it and caressing her flesh as well as the bow.

"Beautiful. But not yet perfect."

He lifted his hands from her, and apparently withdrew something from his coat, for a sparkle caught her eye, a necklace he was lowering in front of her face. She didn't wear much jewelry and didn't have pierced ears. To keep them from healing up quickly, a servant had to wear posts all the time, and she was always too busy to remember to do that, plus sleeping in earrings wasn't comfortable. She'd found it was easiest to pierce her ears each time she wanted to wear them, since it happened so rarely. Plus—the most important reason—the only sharp thing she liked near her ear lobes were Brian's fangs.

The necklace was braided gold and copper, but it was the pendant that caught her eye, a man's ring. As he settled the necklace on her collar bone, she reached up, closed her fingers over the weight of it. She already knew what it was, since he only wore it during formal occasions. He'd never had her wear it, which explained why her heart was pounding like a drum behind her sternum.

It was his family crest. His father had been knighted in England in the 1700s, such that he was as often called *Sir* as *Lord* at vampire gatherings. She particularly liked the design, a green emerald in an antique gold setting that showed a pair of crossed swords and the Latin inscription *Knowledge is Power.*

"My lord…" she said softly, clasping it hard. "What…"

"It works with the dress." He turned her to face him, tracing the cleavage cradling the ring. "And it looks far better there than on my finger."

Her thready breath made her breasts rise beneath his touch. He followed the motion with silent appreciation. "Arch your back for me," he murmured. "Lift them higher, but otherwise stay still."

She bit down on her lip as he cupped one curve, stimulating her nipple below the edge of the low cut neckline with his thumb. Back, forth. Back, forth. It beaded under the thin bra, sent spirals of sensation shooting straight down to her pussy.

"I should have chastised Butch," he said. "These are not tits. A cow has tits. These are breasts. Beautiful, perfect breasts."

"Actually," she said unsteadily, "Cows have teats. Udders."

He arched a brow, nodded, but he kept his eyes on her breasts, watching the reaction of her nipples. "It's interesting how both of them shape to tight points when only one is stimulated. Your whole body connects to one touch, like ripples in a pond."

"Master…" Arousal soaked her panties already. If he kept this up, it would be trickling down her leg.

"That's what I want." His attention flicked up to her face. "And remember, I'll be in your mind tonight. No matter what."

She didn't have the brain cells to explain he needn't trouble himself, that she could handle things. That she just wanted him to forget their earlier exchange about Lord Graham.

"Because if I have to give one minute of thought to your care, I might find you too troublesome?"

"I didn't say—"

"No, you didn't. And I find myself torn between wanting to paddle you to the point of blood for that, and wanting to ask your forgiveness again, for bludgeoning your sense of self-worth such that you don't think you have the right to expect more of me."

He settled his hand on her throat, a light collar above the necklace. While it was difficult to think through that possessive gesture, she struggled for the words. "It's not that. There's no equity in this world, Brian. You made it clear I had to accept that."

"I did. But it's time to reevaluate that, put it in a different context. Yes, in the vampire world, there is no equity between vampires and servants." Backing her against the wall, he put himself up against her. She gasped as he slid his hand between them, beneath the skirt and panties. He began to massage and manipulate her clit and labia with clever fingers that knew everything about her body. "But we're talking about you and me, not the vampire world. What do you want, Debra? I know the answer. I see it in your mind. But I want to hear it from your lips. I want you to speak it out loud to me, not when you think I'm asleep."

He slid his hand from her, brought the fingers to her lips and made her taste herself. "That honey tells me your body is mine. Whenever, however I want it."

Her knees were turning to rubber, but he slid his arm around her waist. "I'm getting older, greedier. I want all of it. I want to push to the bottom of your heart and soul, take over all of it."

"You're scaring me. I'm scared."

He put his lips over hers, his tongue sweeping in to lash and mate with hers. Curving a strong hand over her thigh, he pulled it up to his hip and pushed his erection against her core, let her feel how aroused he already was.

"I want you a little scared, off balance. I want to prove I can be the one that drives the fear away." He bent, took a sharp nip at her throat, licking away the small drops of blood he created.

She wasn't at all sure of this mood. He wasn't Brian, or even Lord Brian. Just simply her Master, and the part of her that wanted to get lost in his commands, desires, was spinning and swirling in a haze.

"Come with me." He straightened, eased back from her, but as he turned to guide her down the hall, he had a steadying hand on the small of her back, his other holding a firm grip on her fingers.

She was glad for his reassuring hold when they turned the corner and she saw Lord Graham emerging from one of the guest rooms. His servant wasn't with him, likely already in the dining room. Servants acquainted themselves informally before their vampires arrived, since they'd be far more intimate with one another as the night progressed.

She regretted the missed opportunity somewhat, but the ability to avert a chance encounter with Graham had compensated for it. Having the steamy encounter with Brian outside her door had exceeded even that.

Besides, she'd already met Dix. Familiarity with the servant of the vampire host helped smooth the way with the others, because he would set the tone. As much as he could, with vampires calling the ultimate shots.

Because of that, she couldn't stop herself from stiffening at the sight of Graham, cold spearing her vitals. But then Brian distracted her entirely.

Putting her up against the wall, he slammed his mouth down on hers. The earlier kiss had been hot, titillating. This was full domination, his hips forced against hers so her body was hiked up the unyielding surface at her back, his cock an iron bar between her legs. Despite the layers of clothing, she ached to be filled by him. Right here, right now. She craved the reminder that she belonged to him alone, that nothing Lord Graham could do to her tonight could touch that.

His hands tangled in her loose hair, thumbs sliding along the corners of her mouth, over her pulse, taking command of all her senses. She let out a tiny, helpless noise as he deepened the kiss. As his arm tightened around her waist, she felt every angle of his body even more acutely.

He didn't stop there. He took over her mind, showing her what he intended to do to her after the dinner was over and they were back in his room. He was going to borrow an ankle spreader bar from Butch's well-equipped dungeon. He would padlock it onto her fine ankles, put her down on her knees in their room, bind her wrists to a leg of the bed. And then he'd take his time, put his mouth on her rim again, use some oil and make her slick before he'd sink his cock to the balls into her ass.

I need to remind you that every orifice, every thought, every desire, belongs to me. I need to fuck your mouth, your cunt and ass, spill my seed on your breasts, inside of you, mark you mine in every way.

God, yes. She couldn't think beyond that.

He kept scrolling those images through her mind. He might take a break after he fucked her ass. Read awhile, make some project notes, all while leaving her bound. Then he'd start all over again, keeping it going until dawn. He'd leave her chained while he slept so her only thought would be of who her Master was. The male who not only held her life in his hand, but her pleasure, her protection, her very happiness.

I want you to look to me for all of it, depend on me for all of it. The way I depend on you for the same things, as well as for more things than I know how to count.

Stunned, she lifted her head when he broke the kiss. Lord Graham could have been perched on the wall behind him like a coven of dragons; she wouldn't have noticed. Her whole world was a pair of vivid eyes, a firm mouth, and the intensity of her Master's thoughts filling her mind.

Despite the chaos of lust and desire surging through her, she snagged on one thing in those thoughts. *You depend on me for your...protection?*

Yes. You protect my sense of myself, Debra. The man and the scientist.

He cradled her jaw in both hands, thumbs stroking her throat, making her lift her chin. His eyes were very close. "There is no one at this dinner but me, Debra. Do you understand? Only my desires, my commands."

He shifted his hips, rubbing his cock with unerring accuracy across her clit, making her thighs loosen further, her breath come faster. "Everything you do will make me desire you more. And whatever you're called to do tonight, your Master will demand even more from you when we close the bedroom door behind us at the end of the evening. Understand?"

"Yes, Master."

Closing his hand on the ring around her neck, he caressed the tops of her breasts with his knuckles. "This is a reminder of who you serve, as much as the third mark you bear."

As she thought about that X-mark branded into her flesh, she suddenly realized it looked like the crossed swords on his crest. Or perhaps she was being fanciful.

"No," he said. "I don't think you are. Because it means you're part of my family."

Her gaze lifted to his. He didn't back away from it, didn't say anything that would explain it any differently, make it acceptable for the vampire-servant relationship. She wanted to protest as she had before, ask him not to do this, but her will was growing weak. Everything he was giving her, piece by piece, was filling that empty part of her she'd reconciled to always being empty.

"Good," he said. "To accomplish that, I'll obliterate your will entirely."

Taking her hand again, he escorted her onward. He took his time, giving her time to slow if not completely calm the spinning of her mind. When he reached the corner where they would be in view of the dining room, she was somewhat steadier. Even so, he stopped, gave her a searching look. He was waiting on her.

Lifting her chin, she met his gaze. "I'm ready, Master," she whispered.

He nodded, touched her face with a look of approval that made her feel she could face anything. Then they stepped around that corner together.

§

Graham reminded her of a serpent. She liked snakes and had no fear of them, having handled plenty growing up on her grandfather's acreage. She remembered shaming a boy she'd liked by scooping up one curled in their path when they were hiking. When she'd relocated the creature out of harm's way, she'd turned to find that same boy had practically leaped fifty feet backwards. "It's just a snake," she'd said, puzzled.

Graham's version of a snake made *her* want to leap back fifty feet. His blue eyes seemed perpetually slitted in calculation, his oval face punctuated by a jutting chin. Lean and sinuous in his movements, he was handsome in a way that seemed...evil to her. As silly as that sounded, her gut told her she was right on target.

Brian was seated across from him. With her standing behind her Master's chair, a servant's normal position at these functions, Graham was in her line of sight. So she focused on Brian's back, the breadth of his shoulders, his hair grazing the collar of his shirt and coat. She could inhale his scent with every breath. He usually wore a light cologne for events such as these, a scent that hinted of smoke and spice.

Confirming Brian was the unofficial guest of honor, Butch had Dix bring the chosen bottle of wine to Brian to sample first. Butch was a known wine connoisseur. As he explained the history and composition of this particular vintage, Dix poured a taste into Brian's glass.

Brian picked up the glass, then lifted a hand out to his side. *Come to me.*

She moved forward, and his fingers closed over her wrist, drawing her to his side. After he tasted the wine, considered it, he drew her down to him. Curving his hand under her hair, he tasted her mouth, the wine still on his. His tongue caressed her lips discreetly, then he drew back. Releasing her nape, he held onto her wrist, thumb stroking her tripping pulse.

"An excellent vintage, my lord. It meshes well with the taste of my servant. I may take a glass to bed at dawn to mix with her blood."

"A good decision." The Texas overlord obviously appreciated her glazed look of arousal and the revealing qualities of her sparkling dress. "I have a couple of wines I particularly enjoy combined with Dix's blood. They're the type of blends that work well with steak and potatoes, since those are the only things he considers food."

Butch gave his servant a fond look. But thanks to Brian's opening volley, the sexual intensity of the room had gone up several notches. She'd hoped for a low key evening in that regard, but with Brian initiating this, her body was humming, eager to see what he might do next.

I like to keep my servant guessing. Your arousal is perfuming the air around my chair.

"I'd enjoy tasting the wine the same way, Lord Brian," Graham noted. His attention felt like he was peeling the clothes off her, evoking far different feelings from Butch or her Master.

"Certainly, Lord Graham." Brian pushed the bottle across the table, a smooth movement that had enough force behind it to require Graham to catch hold of it before it went off the edge and hit the floor. "Your servant looks like her flavor might likewise compliment the taste."

Graham's servant was Jia-Li, a quiet Asian woman who could have been a statue behind the chair. A very beautiful one, her dark hair plaited into a braid that reached her hips. Her silk kimono was sapphire blue with gold embroidery. Her small feet, while not presented in the mutated size of traditionally bound feet, were bound as tightly as possible, apparently to represent the idea for just this night. Debra figured the cramped state must be excruciating. Her own heels were like wearing bedroom slippers in comparison.

She could read nothing from Jia-Li's face, but she sensed no pleasure or arousal from her. Every servant was supposed to come to her vampire willingly, that one choice left up to them, even if all choices were his afterward. But how many of them really knew what it meant until they'd done it? Brian had taken an exceptional risk, letting her know what he was when she was a first mark, giving her the choice before the second mark was given. While she couldn't thank him for everything attendant to that choice, she knew now what a risk he'd taken. Even so, she still wouldn't claim to have truly understood what being a third mark would mean. She wasn't sure any human could, or if it could even be properly explained.

Some things had to be taken on faith.

Brian's fingers tightened infinitesimally on her, but when her lowered gaze shifted toward him, he was carrying on a casual conversation with Butch as if totally unaware of her thoughts. Or his insult to Graham, thwarting his intent. However, she noted the sour look on the California overlord's face. Brian had pissed him off. She couldn't deny a small spurt of satisfaction at it, but the coldness in those snake eyes sent a ripple of dread through her.

Dinner was served, and Brian released her so she could step back behind his chair. Conversation was genial, the three vampires visiting from Butch's territory obviously relaxed and friendly with him, deferential and cordial to Graham.

Two of the three territory vampires were a committed couple, an intriguing and rare dynamic in the vampire world. The pair of male vampires, Tucker and Balen, shared a male servant. Tucker, a sharp-dressed, blue-eyed male with long brown hair like silk, was a lawyer who handled Butch's business interests as his tithe to the overlord. Balen looked like a Viking war lord, with thick red hair cut bluntly to his shoulders. He was a chef in a five-star restaurant in Dallas. A rather appropriate choice, since a vampire could only sample food. Their servant, Reed, a comparatively slender male outfitted in severe black with silver touches on his belt, tie pin and tips of his shoes, was his sous chef.

The other vampire visiting from Butch's territory was female. Tia was a tiny black woman with long red braids like the end of a flogger tied in a top knot on her head, the rest of her cranium bare. She managed a community theater in Houston. Her servant Aila was a slender, comparatively conservative-looking female wearing a sleeveless high-necked dress that nevertheless showed off a pair of magnificent breasts, high and firm, the nipples delineated since she was either wearing an open cup bra or none.

Since Debra had noted everyone in the room appreciating that display, it reinforced what she already knew about vampires. They let their appetites guide them, and if something new was placed on the table, they wouldn't let a simple thing like sexual preference keep them from sampling generously.

She also noticed the three vampires were comfortable with their overlord, jumping into the discussions with Brian to bring up topics along the lines of what Butch had asked earlier. It made sense, them taking advantage of Brian's presence to catch up directly on his research. There was also the usual not-so-subtle pumping for Council information that might affect all their lives.

Brian handled it all with smooth diplomacy. In situations like these his family background always showed. He might prefer to be in his lab with Cheetos and his instruments, but he wasn't a shy or awkward conversationalist. If he'd chosen a different career path, he could have been a diplomat or negotiator. Or even a teacher. He presented information well, without ever sounding condescending. On the contrary; as he spoke about his research, his enthusiasm and excitement often made his audience feel a part of it, which had helped him win support for some of his initially more controversial projects.

A couple of times he asked her to elaborate on some of the things he was discussing. As she approached the table, stood at his side, he linked his hand with hers, caressing her fingers, flustering her no small amount, though she was more than capable of answering their questions. She was an able presenter herself and followed the usual rules about public speaking. She swept her gaze over all the participants, even Graham, though she tried to see him as a blurred face, not registering his features.

Dinner for the vampires was a sampling from a dish that involved fresh beef and a mushroom sauce. It won approval from the chef vampire as well as the rest, the meal coupled with a side of marinated vegetables, finishing up with a berry tart. All of the smells indicated Butch's chef knew his business well. Debra found herself anticipating the meal she and the other servants would have at the conclusion of the evening. She hadn't eaten since Dix's sandwich, her stomach too nervous, but once this was over, it would settle and she'd be ravenous.

Brian pushed back from the table as he finished, dabbing his mouth with a napkin. His significant glance brought her to him once more, and he put her on her knees between his feet. Then he began to feed her, offering her pieces from the mushroom beef dish.

That will keep you on your feet a while longer. Noon is too long to have gone without food. Though I notice you didn't save me any of those pan fried potato chips.

The chips are best when fresh and warm, my lord. I didn't want to give you greasy, stale food.

Perhaps the cook will make me some before dawn. I am the guest of honor, after all.

She lowered her gaze, pressing her lips against a smile. When the house staff came to take away his empty plate, she would have returned to her spot, but he laid a hand on her shoulder. Stroking her collar bone, he played beneath the thin fabric, teasing her bra strap as he resumed his conversation with the other vampires.

The entertainment portion of the evening was closing in fast, where the demands upon her would be far different, and likely far more capricious. In an ideal world, that part of the dinner would be cancelled, and she could just lay her head on her Master's knee, close her eyes and listen to his voice. She wouldn't have to be aware of anyone else at the table.

But this wasn't an ideal world.

"We have a handsome assortment of servants here tonight."

As Butch spoke, the energy in the room changed, sharpened. Brian squeezed her shoulder, but he still didn't bid her rise and take her place behind him. Whether he intended it or not, it emphasized he was with her. She could handle anything.

Yes, you can. I'm very proud of you. Always.

Her hand crept around his ankle, thumb stroking beneath the cuff of his slacks, feeling the network of bones beneath the thin sock.

Butch's gaze slid over all of them, his eyes meeting Debra's briefly. She was aware of Dix's glance as well. "You all know I'm not much on staging a circus performance," the Texas overlord said. He threw a genial look toward Graham, a casual acknowledgement to the other vampire of equal rank at his table. "But I do have a well-equipped dungeon downstairs, and an indoor pool out back. I've found letting servants strip down and play water sports while we enjoy them when and how we wish often has optimal results. It's a warm night, a good night for the pool. It's only five feet, so our lack of buoyancy shouldn't keep you from enjoying it." He slanted a glance at Tia. "I think you might keep your nose above water if you keep on those tall boots of yours."

She scoffed. "Comments like that will ensure my servant keeps her clothes on. And I don't think anyone here wants that."

"No indeed," Dix said, eyeing the large-breasted woman with affectionate appreciation. Aila crossed her eyes at him, earning a grin from the cowboy. They obviously knew one another.

"Typical ranch hand. All you have to do is show him breasts and he's happy." Butch rolled his eyes. "Shall we adjourn to the pool?"

Maybe it was going to be all right. Graham had stayed rather reserved during dinner, and didn't smile at the banter now, but it was clear the others had a familiar relationship. Yet as Brian gave Debra a hand to her feet and turned to push in the chair, she unfortunately met Graham's gaze. He showed her the tips of his fangs, eyes glittering.

She started, bumping into Brian.

Damn it, damn it, *damn it*. She'd resolved not to show him an ounce of reaction. Though the opportunity was lost, she made herself give him a cordial nod. Graham's lips quirked at her sham, mocking her.

She genuinely hated him. His smugness, his cruelty, his very existence.

Easy. Brian spoke in her mind, his hand on her lower back. He guided her out the dining room and through the patio, headed for the pool. She put her hand over his on her hip, holding onto her Master. It might be pathetic, but she was going to take the lifeline he'd offered her. To be with her through this, through every step.

"It's not pathetic at all." Brian's lips brushed her ear, his arm banding around her waist. "It's what you should expect from me."

The pool was lotus-shaped and the size of two Olympic ones. A lazy river formed a border around it, passing beneath a mushroom-shaped waterfall. There was a slide, an adjoining salt water spa and hot tub. Scattered around the pool were lounge chairs, as well as an assortment of foam water toys, paddle boards, a volleyball net and other games.

But that wasn't all the pool area had to offer. Butch opened up a cabinet full of waterproof sex toys and water-friendly restraint options, including floating rafts equipped with Velcro straps. Hoses with adjustable pressure settings in easy reach of the pool side provided some further intriguing possibilities, and the several diving boards possessed eye hooks beneath, so a servant could be tied and suspended at various heights above and in the water.

"Have fun, kids," he advised. Then he glanced at Dix. "Get the ball rolling, boy."

Dix stripped off his clothes with no modesty, revealing densely packed muscle on his lean form from shoulders to calves. With a yell, he did a cannonball, showering Butch with water. Butch held his wine out to the side, sparing it a chlorine dip, and shook his head. "Now I'll have to go teach him some respect," he said with mock disgust.

The other servants had begun to shed their clothes. At Brian's nod, Debra started to do the same, sliding her dress off her shoulder. Brian's gaze followed the descent, lingering on her breasts and the curve of her waist, but Butch nudged him.

"You can look at her in a minute. You wanted me to point out some of the significant topography, things that indicate the geological history of the area. You can see it pretty good from this vantage point…"

Butch drew her Master out to the patio with him, though Brian gave her a bolstering, heated look that suggested he wouldn't be gone long. Tucker and Tia joined them. Debra let out a steadying breath as she unhooked her bra, let it slide down her arms. This type of set up was usually the best case scenario for her, the vampires engaged in networking and social conversation while the servants served as eye candy. It allowed friendlier, more informal interaction between the servants.

Proving the point, Dix had already positioned the volleyball net and was gesturing to Debra to come join in on a game. She saw with some surprise Balen, the chef vampire, preferred to join them and his servant Reed in the game rather than join the other vampires. He and the sous chef traded insults in a way that reminded her of Butch and Dix. It was interesting how the lead vampire's behavior tended to influence those who followed him. She thought of Lyssa and Jacob, and that fertility report. She might be wary about hoping too much for her own situation, but as a scientist she could tell the markers of change.

Then there were those who refused to change.

Graham was over by the wet bar, making himself a drink. He'd ordered Jia-Li to take off her clothes as well. But when she moved toward the wall to balance herself on her hampered feet, he made a sharp movement that said he expected her to take off her clothes where he bid her. Which made her dilemma obvious.

She couldn't balance herself. At her first attempt, she toppled, landing on one knee on the concrete before she could catch herself with her hands. He gave her a disdainful, bored look. "Again. Until you get undressed standing on your own feet."

He'd caught Dix's attention. Debra saw the man's countenance darken at the display, but he knew as well as she did a servant couldn't interfere between a vampire and his servant. Only a higher-ranking vampire could, and most didn't. Objections from another servant only made it worse for the servant suffering. There were plenty more Grahams in the vampire world than Lady Lyssas.

The sous chef called Dix's name. He lifted a reluctant shoulder in acknowledgment, turning back to the pool.

This time when Jia-Li fell, Graham kicked her side. "Do it again," he said between his teeth, "And it will be your face."

Dix turned at that, his eyes flashing. She saw Balen mutter something, a sharp warning. Dix twitched at it, and Reed ducked under the net, coming quietly to his side, putting a hand on his arm. Graham was oblivious to it, thank goodness, but if he kicked her again…she had a feeling Dix wasn't going to be held back.

This was her fault. Brian had denied Graham a simple touch of his mouth on her arm, to protect her feelings. Now his servant was taking the brunt of his anger. Debra knew the signs of a servant who enjoyed being humiliated. The only emotion Jia-Lia exuded was stoic endurance.

Butch and Brian were back on the patio. She heard a snippet

about California landscapes, fossilized layers, and then Butch called out to Graham. Graham gave his servant one last ominous look, a promise that the kick in the face would come later, even if he had no time to attend to it now.

The woman was getting up again, but it was obvious he'd given her a task whose only outcome was failure. Debra's fingers curled and uncurled. Of all the things she didn't want to do in the world, drawing Graham's attention ranked at the top. But when Jia-Li started to lose her balance again, Debra was already moving.

She thought of all the things she'd internalized about vampires and servants. If she gripped that experience in both hands, made it work for her, she might empower herself, take a giant step toward the place those far more comfortable with this had reached. She'd chosen this world for Brian, yes. But he'd known the depths of her submissive nature, had known a part of her craved the challenge of serving him in a world where sexual dominance was explored in such uninhibited ways. She'd only stumbled because she'd expected to always have him at her side, at her back, leading her.

But wasn't that a two-way street? A submissive had the power to call a Master to her, if she chose to claim that power. She could anticipate his needs and enjoy the challenge of catering to them in creative ways. And as far as other vampires were concerned, most weren't like Graham, craving a servant's fear and pain far past the pleasure threshold. She could use her considerable brain to turn the situation in a different direction. Most vampires wanted to arouse their servants, feed off their pleasure.

As the vampires moved back into the pool area, she noticed Brian's attention immediately returned to her. It seemed like a punctuation mark to her thoughts.

This time as Jia-Li toppled, Debra caught her. She had a third mark's strength. She could hold a woman in her arms as securely as a mortal male, keep her upright. Jia-Li was a tiny thing like Tia, barely five feet tall herself.

"Don't," the woman muttered.

"Sssh," Debra said. She slid behind Jia-Li, keeping her arms around her. Once there, she placed her lips on her lightly powdered throat. Then her teeth, stroking that SCM with her tongue. She smiled against Jia-Li's flesh, remembering the erotic anatomy lesson. "Lean against me," she whispered.

As she'd anticipated, she'd caught pretty much every vampire's attention, as well as the servants'. Those in the pool drifted to the side to watch.

She figured out how to remove the kimono, and the undergarments followed. She folded the silk garment carefully over a lounge chair, keeping her hand on the other servant. Jia-Li had scars on her back, long stripes that had to have been incurred tonight. They were healing slowly because her Master had not provided her the blood needed to make them disappear. Some vampires liked to do that, an accessory for the evening like jewelry. Some servants liked showing off such marks. She didn't think Jia-Li was one of them.

She drew the woman back against her, cradling her small breasts in her hands, nipping her throat along the hair line of her silky black mane. "Your hair is so beautiful," she murmured. "Like a cloak if you unbraided it."

Despite her initial trepidation, Jia-Li proved she was experienced enough to pick up on Debra's intent. Reaching back to clasp Debra's hips, she rotated her backside against Debra's mound with a skillful stroke.

As Brian and Butch settled in lounge chairs to watch, Graham sank down in one to Butch's left, his gaze narrowed. For all Graham knew, Brian had told her to do this, so if they managed a distracting enough display, she could avert Jia-Li being punished for disobedience.

Jia-Li was fine-boned and lovely as a doll. Turning her to face her, Debra tangled her fingers with hers, backed her up to the wet bar. Then she lifted her up onto one of the stools. Pulling her own hair over one shoulder to keep it out of the way, she bent to kiss the woman's thigh, curling her hands over both her knees to spread them wide, show the bare pussy between her thighs. Jia-Li's eyes met hers, then her lashes lowered.

Debra wondered what Brian was thinking. A sidelong glance showed him as intrigued by two women pleasuring each other as any man here. It almost made her smile, despite her serious intent. As she worked her way up Jia-Li's thigh, she embraced that hum of sensation that said she had his full presence in her mind, and spoke to it.

Too bad we can't take her into your bed tonight, my lord. You could sample some wine off her smooth, pretty pussy. I could take your cock in my mouth. Then

I could straddle you, take you inside me, and put her in front of me. I'd cup her breast, capture her nipple between my knuckles and squeeze. Slide my fingers into all the wetness I can smell now, make her come as you command it. All while you fucked me, making me beg for release…

She was arousing herself and feeling a power from it, a much more refreshing feeling than fear. Heat washed over her as her Master responded.

As pleasurable as that sounds, I prefer having my servant bear the weight of all my desires. I'll sip wine off every inch of her skin until she's trembling, mindless and begging.

Anything you desire is my pleasure, Master.

She pulled two cushions off a nearby chair to give her the height she needed to kneel. But before she did, she laid her hand on Jia-Li's sternum, spreading out her fingers so they could caress her small breasts. Applying pressure, she made the woman lean back against the bar, then further, until her shoulder blades were against the flat surface, her head tipped back, which made her thrust her breasts upward and tilt her hips.

The dominant gesture had Jia-Li's eyes sparking. This woman was a true submissive like Debra, but not the kind who responded to brutality like Graham's. Debra wondered how he'd tricked her into believing otherwise. At least she could give her the right treatment tonight.

"Stay right like that," she said softly. "Or I'll stop."

Jia-Li didn't smile. She'd probably forgotten how the first week in Graham's service, but Debra saw the flicker of need in her gaze. She could help her get lost in it.

In her peripheral vision, Dix and the other two servants were leaning on the pool lip, watching. The chef vampire was sitting on the ledge, his servant pressed against his leg. Tucker and Tia sat together on her left, Brian, Graham and Butch just behind her and to her right, their eyes gleaming in the shadows of the dimly lit pool area. She and Jia-Li were center stage, and she knew what was required for that.

She blocked out Graham. He didn't exist. Only her Master existed. This was for him, and the more she pleasured him the more she'd pleasure herself, a never-ending circle.

Putting her hands on the Asian woman's thighs, she spread her out wider, moved between them. Jia-Li had a scent like jasmine oil flavored with vanilla. It was a nice combination. Debra nuzzled her upper thighs, kissed the soft skin, moved closer to the woman's cunt, sensing Jia-Li's breath hitching, her fingers closing into tense knots at her side. When Debra finally closed her mouth over her, giving her one thorough, long lick from clit to perineum, teasing the petals in between with an artful swirl of her tongue, Jia-Li shuddered, an intense, compact response that reminded Debra of a seismic tremor coming from within the earth.

How long it had been since Graham had allowed her to take pleasure from her service? That was one thing Brian always did. Whatever else he demanded of her, when they came together like this, he made sure Debra saw stars.

She traced Jia-Li's pussy with her tongue and then thrust inside, using her hands to caress the flexing muscles of the woman's thighs. But something wasn't quite right. Jia-Li's pleasure was being disrupted by discomfort. Her bound feet. Well, Graham had ordered her to undress, hadn't he?

Debra lifted her head. Stroking Jia-Li's straining abdomen, she gripped her waist, a light pressure telling the woman she wanted her to straighten. As she did, Debra's hand slipped to her hips and back to her knees. Sinking to a full seat on her heels, she clasped one of the other servant's ankles. She slid off the tiny shoe into which Jia-Li's bound foot had been forced. Fortunately Graham hadn't required her to break the arch or toes to fit into typical lotus foot mold, a painful process requiring far more than a night to accomplish for a mortal. When she'd traveled with Brian in Japan, she'd seen a few elderly women who bore the permanent disability the fashion had inflicted upon them.

This wasn't that severe, thank goodness, but Debra still winced at the tight arch the bindings had forced Jia-Li to endure. As she freed Jia-Li's cramped toes from the wrappings, she wondered that she could walk at all. She massaged the toes and the arch as long as she dared. Not wanting Graham to interfere if he thought cosseting Jia-Li had become more important than entertaining their audience, Debra bent to place her lips on one foot. She knew all the erogenous zones associated with that area, because Brian could use fingers, lips, tongue and fangs in artful ways that made every touch shoot sensation straight up the inside of her thighs. When he finally did close his mouth over her pussy, Debra usually came instantly.

She'd obviously learned well from his tutelage. In no time, Jia-Li's response had her arched back over the bar, soft gasps coming from her lips. Debra lifted Jia-Li's ankles, guiding her legs so they slid over Debra's shoulders. She stayed on her knees but lifted off of her heels, adjusting her knees outward in a sinuous movement that telegraphed her awareness of her audience. She was still wearing the scrap of panties, so as she bent forward, she arched her back, lifting her hips so her Master was getting a view of her plump, silk-covered sex, the crotch wet from all the things she was thinking about and doing for him.

Jia-Li's pussy was glistening from Debra's attentions, and Debra intended for her to get even wetter. As Debra started licking and sucking on her pussy again, the other woman's fingers scraped the bar surface. When she started thrusting with her tongue, Debra was conscious of her own body responding to the stimulation, her ass lifting higher and then lowering, her body mimicking the act of being fucked. Brian wouldn't take her now, wouldn't block the show for others, but she wanted him to see what she wanted, that she was ready for him whenever he desired. She became more enthusiastic in her ministrations, her breasts quivering with her movements, and knew he'd be looking at them as well.

He hadn't spoken in a while, but the heat on her flesh, unfurling inside her, told her she had his full attention, his mind inside her mind. He was with her.

She wanted to feel Jia-Li's climax, wanted to claim that power for herself. She didn't have long to wait.

Jia-Li shuddered and began to come, a silent, intense event where her body convulsed and gasping moans had to tear themselves from her constricted throat. She might be punished for it, but that didn't really matter, did it? This was just a shelter in an ongoing storm for her. Debra redoubled her efforts, making sure she gave the woman as much pleasure as she could.

As the woman rocked to completion against Debra's mouth, she was making a barely audible keening noise. Glancing up the slope of her body, Debra saw her chest rising and falling quickly, as if she were close to some type of emotional break. Debra made a soothing sound, stroking her stomach, her hips and her thighs with gentle fingertips. Fortunately, the vampires remained silent, watching, no interruption as of yet. As Jia-Li's breath steadied, Debra rose, curled a hand around her waist and helped her sit up. She put her arms around Jia-Li, held her.

I wish I could make this better for you. For more than this moment.

She couldn't say it aloud, because vampire hearing was far too sharp. But Jia-Li had more spirit than she'd expected. Debra drew in a breath as Jia-Li's mouth closed over her nipple and started to suckle with a provocatively strong pull. Her small hands came around to cup Debra's buttocks, stroke her curves. In her current aroused state, Debra was more than willing to lean into the stimulation.

"Stop."

Jia-Li stiffened at Graham's command. Her head lifted, expressive eyes meeting Debra's before sweeping down again. Debra heard the creak of the chair as Graham rose, felt his ominous heat as he approached. She steeled herself to immobility as he curled a fingertip around her hair. In the corner of her gaze, she saw him staring at his servant. Jia-Li kept her lashes lowered.

"Your servant did that so very well, Lord Brian," Graham said. "I expect you'd have no objection if I put her mouth to more strenuous use. I'd like to see her do the same for the rest of us. See if she can be as courteous and generous to the men as she is with women. Starting with me."

Asking was a courtesy. Brian was neither overlord nor Region Master, nor in line for either post. Graham had every right to demand it, and there was nothing her Master could do.

Her sense of empowerment fled, replaced by fear and loathing. The memories of all those other times he'd forced her to do his bidding flooded her mind, paralyzing her. But she fought the feeling back. She wouldn't shame her Master. He'd asked her for her trust, and she'd take that leap now. Even if he disappointed her again afterward, it would still help her get through this.

She straightened, faced Graham. "Whatever my Master wills. I enjoy serving his pleasure."

Graham's visible surprise gave her a surge of triumph. She'd done it. She'd shown him nothing on which he could feed. She actuallycould do it, immerse herself in her desire for Brian to make it work. She would remain untouched in mind or spirit by this monster's use of her body.

"No," Brian said.

Chapter Eight

The sexual tension swirling through the room was cut like a rope. Butch set aside his wine, straightening in his chair, but Brian had already risen from his. He came to her side and faced Graham. As he did, he placed a hand on her shoulder. Obeying the unspoken command, she sank to her knees at his side, lowering her head.

I can do this, Master. It's all right. I shouldn't have made you feel—

I didn't ask your opinion, Debra. Be still.

It startled her, his tone as imposing as she'd ever heard it. When she dared a glance up, the look on his face was…dangerous. Earlier she'd thought he reminded her of his father. This wasn't his father or anyone else. It was even more than the male who'd conquered her in so many delicious ways.

What she saw in his face and felt through his touch was pure vampire. A creature who didn't consider dominance a negotiation, but something he would fight or kill for if necessary. It was a thrilling look for him. And terrifying, since the vampire he was facing was far more powerful.

Graham's lip curled back, fangs elongating so the sharp tips gleamed. Dix pulled himself out of the pool in a lithe move, water sluicing from his bare body as he joined Butch, who was also on his feet. The other servants had likewise moved to their Masters and Mistress, an acknowledgement that violence might be about to ensue and of their proper place in such a situation. In a heartbeat, everything had changed, because of a two-letter word never said by a lower-ranked vampire. Or a servant, for that matter. *No.*

"I don't think I heard you correctly," Graham said, those snake's eyes narrowing further.

"You certainly did. Vampires don't suffer from impaired hearing." Brian's gaze remained steady, cold. "I am denying you the use of my servant, my lord, and asking you to respect my reasons for doing so. She has exceeded expectations with her performance, and there are other ways to enjoy the servants that are here. I claim her for myself alone for the rest of the night."

"You don't have that right. You don't have the rank to do it."

"Yes, I do."

Debra saw the other vampires exchange glances. Butch's attention remained fixed on Graham, his visage unreadable.

"I am Director of the Vampire Council Research Center," Brian said, "and a valued advisor to Lady Lyssa, the head of the Vampire Council. I'm the vampire responsible for a cure to the Delilah virus, and making significant advances on resolving vampire fertility issues, the two major threats to our species. Those contributions have earned me a rank that allows me to say no to you, Lord Graham. She's mine, and it is up to me how I wish to share her."

"You're bluffing. And you've gone soft over your servant." Graham sneered. "A crime that carries severe punishment. It could get her killed."

"Only if my dead body is part of that equation." Though Brian's tone remained mild, his eyes sharpened to knife blade precision.

"Sounds like she owns you, rather than the other way around."

"Those scientific advances are as much her accomplishment as mine," Brian said flatly. "She has served our species in ways no other servant has, and asked nothing from it except wanting to serve a Master worthy of her. I haven't lived up to my part of the bargain on that, but that will not be the case tonight."

His lip curled back, his fangs showing sharp and deadly. "She is my servant, Lord Graham. Mine, not because I took her by force or tricked her, but because she surrendered her heart and soul to me willingly, believing I would be *worth* her freedom. Worth giving up any life other than to be my servant."

The shock of it had her forgetting protocol. She raised her head, stared at his profile. His fingers tightened on her shoulder, even as he kept his gaze locked on Graham. "When a brilliant, strong woman gives you a gift like that, you damn well better be deserving of it. Which means if you lay a finger or any other appendage on her, I swear to every god of substance that you *will* lose them."

He released her, but only to shift so he put himself directly between her and Graham. It put the two vampires nearly chest to chest. "So am I bluffing, Lord Graham?"

Amazement flashed back to fear. She didn't want him hurt. The room was humming with impending violence. Her mind sifted through possibilities, contingencies, ways to head off a direct conflict, but came up against a wall. There was nothing she could do here.

This was between the two vampires.

The room was silent, tense, everyone waiting for Graham's next move. After a long moment, Graham sneered again, shifted his body away from Brian's, putting some space between them. Not a retreat, though. He turned toward Butch. "While my young friend has forgotten protocol, I have not. As host and overlord of the ground on which we're standing, you have the right to make the call on this." Graham's gaze sharpened. "Though I advise you to choose wisely, Butch."

Debra dared a look past Brian's hip. Butch lifted a brow at the implied threat, but otherwise his stone expression gave nothing away, his gray eyes glittering. Brian's attention remained fixed on Graham. Though not so much as a twitch suggested his awareness of anyone else in the room, Debra felt her Master's heat in her mind like a furnace.

Butch considered the two potential combatants, then his gaze swept the pool area. All three vampires from his territory were silent, but Debra noticed they were all looking to Butch. Their loyalty wasn't toward Graham. Which was probably why Graham had chosen the political route, knowing that to start a fight to the death in his host's home might have far more negative consequences.

"I think this is going to get really messy unless you concede the point," Butch said at last. His piercing gray eyes conveyed a wealth of messages as they met Graham's gaze. "He's not playing. Let it go. He's right. There are plenty other ways to seek pleasure tonight. If the man isn't in a sharing mood, that's his call."

"But his rank—"

"I'm not in a position to dispute it," Butch responded shortly. "But I do believe he's correct. Based on his current position with Council, he likely outranks everyone here. Take it up with him when he falls out of favor. For now, let's not piss him off. He might inject a virus in the pool and make all our dicks fall off."

Chuckles rippled through the group, easing some of the tension. Debra remained wary though, taking her cue from Dix. His gaze on Butch remained serious and still. This wasn't over yet.

Graham's lips twisted, and he inclined his head, albeit ungraciously. "I will take my leave, Lord Dorn. It seems I'm not compatible with the current company."

Butch shrugged. "Suit yourself. But nobody likes a sore loser,

Graham. You'd do better to stay and make a better accounting of yourself than getting your rocks off torturing female servants."

Graham's face froze. As Butch stepped forward, closing the distance between him and the other vampire, the overlord looked far less friendly. The "good old boy" mien vanished, replaced by a look which explained exactly why he was an overlord. Most came to it by a combination of strategic politicking, brute force and kissing the ass of the right vampires. Based on his next words, Debra was pretty sure Butch had only used the first two methods.

"The world is changing," Butch said softly. "Catch up, or you'll see the sun a lot sooner than the rest of us. Count on it."

With a snarl, Graham pivoted and marched from the room. Jia-Li gave Debra another nod, picked up her kimono and went after him. Debra watched her, her heart hurting, wishing she could have helped more. But Jia-Li's choice had been made, as hers had.

Glancing up at the profile of her Master, she was glad she'd chosen better. With the potential threat dissipated, Brian's words were sinking in, leaving her more than a little stunned. He'd just become one of a very small handful of vampires who'd publicly championed his servant, making it clear a Master had the right to protect his servant, keep her exclusive when he so desired, at his discretion. And he'd had the rank—or the poker face—to pull it off.

Her heart was tripping, her throat was thick. When Brian stepped back, put his hand on her shoulder again, slid his fingers along her nape, the touch undid her. She bowed her head, closing her eyes at the feeling.

My servant won't look at me?

She didn't want the others see how overwhelmed she was. His fingers stroked her again, a gentle insistence. But Butch came to Brian's side then, giving her a moment's reprieve. The Texas overlord touched her cheek with a fingertip, a surprising acknowledgement, then he addressed Brian.

"Well, damn. I was going to have her suck me off too, and you've just ruined it. If he hears you let me have her and not him, he'll be pissing and moaning until Christmas."

Despite her unbalanced state, Debra's gaze flicked up in time to see the twinkle in the overlord's gaze. But there was a serious message under his tone, and Brian didn't miss it.

"I apologize, my lord," he said formally. "While I don't regret the act, I didn't mean to cause discord while under your hospitality."

Butch nodded, accepting the courtesy, but he shrugged. "He was the one being an ass. Come on, enough of this shit. You and your servant are free to enjoy the pool however you want. Let's relax and get some enjoyment out of one another's company before the dawn sends us to bed."

With that, the overlord moved off, already shedding his shirt. Conversations resumed, and then the servants were back in the pool, Dix recovering the volley ball despite Reed's best attempt to grab it. Butch paused at the pool's edge, addressing his three territory vampires in a low voice. They glanced toward Brian. Debra noted smiles at whatever Butch said. Tia looked openly relieved, the men more relaxed. Their looks held speculation, but the overall energy felt all right, especially when the other vampires shed their clothes and joined their overlord in the pool.

Only then did Brian's shoulders ease. Whatever immediate challenges might result from his actions had passed, and her Master could now relax as well. Sliding his hand from her bare shoulder to her elbow, he brought her to her feet, tipping up her chin with his finger.

"You will look at me now," he ordered quietly.

When she did, she found herself unable to say anything. Her mind and heart were torn between two possibilities. Tonight he'd made it clear which path was truth, but for so long, she'd had to believe in far less, accept that as the best she could hope to have from him.

Brian shook his head and drew her out to the patio. Sinking down in a chair, he pushed her onto the foot stool before him, stroking a hand through her hair. He didn't say anything for a bit, and the rhythmic motion, his thoughtful gaze, steadied her enough to be practical, to think of the more important issues that had been raised.

"My lord, what you said...do you think it was wise? I don't want your research to be jeopardized." *Or your life.*

He caught her hand, brushed his lips over her knuckles before squeezing them. "It's something I should have said and done a long time ago. A life half lived isn't worth living. You are my other half, Debra. A true partner in every way."

Her heart and soul simply stopped. She swayed and he dropped his touch to her hips, steadying her.

"Ssshh," he murmured. "It's all right. Don't faint on me."

Despite his grim humor, she gripped his elbows, stared into his face. "I don't understand…why…what happened?"

He sobered. "I had to face the possibility of losing you that night, with Gideon. It unlocked something inside me I've kept locked down for far too long. Tonight it came to a head."

He traced her cheek, her lips. "We've always had an unconventional vampire-servant relationship, because we work together. But I allowed that to blind me to my responsibilities as your vampire master."

His expression steeled in a way that had her straightening under his hands, a nervous flutter in her lower belly. "In the future," he said, "if you have a problem with a vampire like Graham, and if I am too caught up in my work to notice, you will bring it to my attention. I have great faith in your judgment, Debra. I trust you won't make the serious error of deciding it's not something I need to be bothered about. Else I will find a memorable way to correct that impression."

His even look made her toes curl. "And if I am not strong enough to protect you from whatever comes our way," he added, "I will take the time-honored geek tradition of availing myself of my far more physical friends. They owe me large favors, and, with the help of your exceptional mind, I intend that beneficial situation to continue to exist, far into our future together."

She was caught between a smile and much stronger emotions. Despite the fact he sat before her fully dressed and she was in nothing but a scrap of underwear, she felt cloaked in his love and protection, in need of no other covering. At the thought, his gaze became even more vibrant. But then it shadowed.

"I've never offered you the choice, Debra. It's been there, available to you for these past couple of years. You helped me create it, could have asked for it at any time."

He was talking about the Cleves serum, which removed a vampire's marks. Her stomach tilted, suddenly knowing where he was going with this. She started to draw back, stand, but he caught her hands, held her firmly in place.

"In the human world, you'd be at the top of your field. Here, no matter what advances we make, you will always be considered first and foremost a vampire's servant." He touched her chin. "I could delve to the bottom of your soul and never unravel the mystery of why you made that choice. Why you continue to make it. I only know

I am grateful for it like nothing else in my life."

Tears pricked her eyes. But he wasn't done.

"That gratitude will never change," he said. "However, from now until the end of your life, I'm giving you the choice all servants are told they don't have, once they decide to serve. The choice of changing your mind."

That serum also came with a memory-eraser, a charged potion that had blended science and magic, thanks to the help of a human sorcerer, a Guardian of the Light known to Lord Mason. But to not remember Brian, any of this…

He shook his head. "Lyssa and the Council would agree to let me do it without the memory removal. You have earned our trust many times over, plus the foundation of knowledge you carry might be of use to the vampire world in the future. I know your heart. I know you would help us if there was need. I will let you go, Debra, if that's what you want."

The sincerity in his gaze, the earnest intensity…this was the male who'd offered to make her his servant, who'd urgently wanted her to make that choice. Now that his heart was in his eyes, she saw she hadn't been wrong about him. Or her choice.

That truth filled her, so that for a moment she couldn't even speak. She put her head down on his shoulder, clung to his shoulders, just breathed. Tried to breathe. He pressed his lips to her temple, her bare shoulder. Stroked her back. "Debra."

She lifted her head, touched his face. "Don't you remember what I said when I was talking to my grandfather about meeting you? You were everything I'd ever wanted. Someone who challenged my mind. Who made my knees weak, who made me want you with every breath."

"That's a gift that goes both ways." He brushed his lips over hers, stayed so close his eyes dominated her vision. "Before I made you my servant, I saw my more primal vampire urges as…not an embarrassment exactly, but not something I'd explored." His eyes glinted. "By making you mine, I discovered that side of myself. I suppressed it, out of some mistaken belief that I was giving in to my impulses too much, endangering my plans for a facility…endangering you, if I made the mistake of allowing myself to get too besotted with you. I saw such passionate feelings as a growing pain, a young vampire's mistake, instead of what it truly was. Letting myself fall in love."

Her heart rate accelerated at the forbidden words, even as his fingers circled her wrist, stroked that rapid pulse, steadied it.

"But," he added, with emphasis, "I don't want you to think of my feelings, but your own. This is not the career or relationship you envisioned having."

No. That was certainly true. She met his gaze, saw it darken with the pain of her thought. "Do you remember Lord Theo?" she asked. "When he contracted the Delilah virus, he chose to die with his servant, rather than taking the cure, letting her sacrifice her life for him. The ironic thing is he opposed Lyssa's stance on giving servants more protection and rights. But when it came to his own servant...he refused to relinquish his connection to her. She told him she would take the serum, allow him to live. He told her he was worried if their connection was severed by death, he wouldn't find her in the afterlife, and he refused to let her go."

When his brow creased, she shook her head. "What I'm trying to say is it's very hard to understand what love is, my lord. And focusing on what I might accomplish for myself, the recognition I receive, is not the same as the deed itself, the results of it. I may not have envisioned you as the male of my dreams, or this as my career, but before you, I imagined love according to the experiences of the human world. You opened me up to far deeper things that I wanted, that weren't part of that world. I didn't make the wrong choice. I have *never* regretted it."

Now he was the one who looked surprised. She felt him probing her mind for the truth of it, and saw the change in his face as he realized she meant it. She trembled at that look.

"I have simply longed for more," she whispered. "That was the source of my unhappiness, thinking I could never have all of you that I desired. I could not possibly leave you, my lord." She reached up, framed his face with her hands again. "You are my Master, my heart and soul. Just fill them with yourself and your desires, and I will never regret anything but not having all eternity to be with you."

The words made her twice as vulnerable as she'd been the night she'd told him she loved him. But everything he'd done these past few days, and especially tonight, had given her the confidence to hope. To believe.

His hands tightened on her, a silent acknowledgment of her

thoughts. Then he drew her up to kiss her mouth, her eyelashes, her forehead, his arms sliding around her, pulling her even closer between his spread thighs on the chair. She dug her fingers into his back until he broke the kiss, pressed her head to his shoulder and just held her. She thought the world could turn forever and she'd be content just like this.

But her Master had a way of always giving her more delicious things to want.

"And just what does my servant want now?"

She smiled against his shoulder, lifted her head to stroke a hand through his thick hair. "It's something best demonstrated, my lord."

The flare of interest in his gaze told her she had his leave to continue. She slid her hands beneath his coat, pushed it off his shoulders. He helped her, shrugging out of it as she left him to that and began to open the shirt down the front, caressing his chest as she did so. Her fingers rested briefly on his sternum, trailed down to the base of it. "I have a great deal of interest in the superficial front line myself, my lord."

"Hmm." He pursed his lips. "But the superficial front line skips a key area I feel will require in-depth attention. With your mouth, your hands…"

She grinned and pushed the shirt off his shoulders as well, letting her fingertips linger on the fine architecture of bone and muscle. Crowding closer to him brought her breasts against his bare chest. She let out a tiny sigh at the wondrous feel of it. He clasped her waist in strong hands.

"You wanted me to fill you with my desires," he observed. "Just how much filling do you need?"

"I'm not sure, my lord. Perhaps you could just keep filling the cup until I say stop."

He chuckled at that, then he cinched her close, lifting her to her feet as he rose so her toes didn't touch the ground when he kissed her. "And another thing," he added. "You will never attend another vampire event without me. Period."

She thought it might be possible to shatter from such an overload of feeling, too much to process.

"Nothing to process tonight. Just feel, Debra." He met her lips in another wine-saturated kiss. This one had an even sweeter wine with it, such that she curled her fingers in his biceps, held on, delighted as he made the kiss so long, the world just swirled away.

When he finally lifted his head, let her feet touch, she was breathless, but his eyes gleamed in that way she'd learned to anticipate with delicious anxiety. "I think I do want to enjoy the water with my servant." His gaze slid down to the panties. "But she's overdressed."

He still wore the belted slacks, his shoes. "Same goes, Master."

He gave her a mock stern look, but hooked his thumbs in the thong himself, had her step out of it as he went to his heels and let her hold onto his shoulder to steady herself. The contrast between that and Graham kicking Jia-Li for being unable to stand on contorted feet underscored the difference between the two vampires, and demonstrated in one act all the promises Brian had just made to her. Her eyes stung with tears, but she battled them back. She wanted this to be all about pleasure.

She drew in a breath as he bent and lifted her in his arms, carrying her through the patio door and toward the pool. He didn't carry her often. She liked it.

I'll do it so often you'll tire of it.

She doubted that could ever happen.

When he used the zero entry slope to walk them into a curve of the lotus-shaped pool, she found the water a pleasant temperature, neither too cold nor too hot. Her Master let her down, but he backed her toward one of the rafts that had been tossed into this end of the pool, tangling his hands with hers as he maneuvered her toward it. Then he scooped her against him with one arm, the two of them drifting in circles as he kissed her, let her twine her legs around him. She let all the fears go, let herself be swamped by love for him.

As she'd told him, her pain and regret came not from the choice itself, but in longing for the choice to live up to her expectations. This moment exceeded them. Then he took it even further.

He opened his mind to her.

Not just the surface level where they solved research problems. His heart and soul, where she could sense the collection of feelings gathered there. This was new for him, too, allowing himself to express his feelings for her, rather than being focused on suppressing them. And he wondered why he'd ever done anything different.

This feeling is worth dying for, Debra. That's what Lyssa and Jacob knew, and why they chose not to hide it.

She couldn't agree more. The water should have concealed her tears, but he kissed every one of them amid the water droplets. The raft was against her back, a cushion between her and the pool wall, not that she would have even noticed the scrape of the concrete with his mouth on her. But then Brian lifted her onto the raft and tender emotion became something else.

It was one of the inflatable rafts outfitted with four Velcro cuffs. Her Master's order came through her mind, along with a surge of erotic intent. *Lay your arms out to your sides and spread your legs.*

It was like being on a waterbed, the gentle roll and bob. He held it steady as she complied, his heated attention sliding over her naked form. It made her body dampen and tighten for him in ways he could see, scent. Those hazel eyes reflecting the pool lights became even more silver-green, and she trembled under his touch when he wrapped the cuffs around her wrists and ankles. If the raft turned over, she would be face down, trapped, unable to breathe. While technically that couldn't kill a fully marked servant, she could lose consciousness, experience the same panic that any mortal could. But she wasn't worried. Her Master was with her, caring for her.

Brian caressed her calf. He drew the raft over to the steps so he could take a seat on one, a position that let him lean over her and touch her how he desired. She bit her lip as he traced her breast, flicking a nipple taut from the cool touch of the water. Then he slid down and cupped her between her legs, slipping his fingers into her. She lifted her hips to him, responding to the penetration, the stroking touch. When he withdrew, he slicked the fluid gathered on his fingers over her outer labia. She trembled, eager to serve him. Eager to please.

He'd been the first to understand that she wasn't two separate entities. There was the driven, detail-oriented scientist who spent whatever time or energy was necessary to solve a puzzle, the one who would fight for the theories she knew were right and worth pursuing, whether she was at the bottom of the totem pole in the first lab she'd worked, or arguing a point last week with the vampire who'd made her his servant. But that woman was the same as this one. The all-the-way-to-her-soul submissive who hungered to tear herself open and give herself completely to one Master. The Master touching her now.

He pressed his fingers back inside her, deeper this time. Finding the right places to stroke, make her come apart. "Completely, hmm? Tell me. Out loud."

"Yes, Master. Everything. I'm…yours." She panted over the words as his clever fingers worked her, had her shuddering and twitching on the raft. Brian rose then, keeping his hand in her as he used the other to move them out of the lotus pool into the flow of the lazy river. He kept pace with her in the current, holding onto the raft with one hand, still playing with her pussy with the other. She moistened her lips, heard the rush of water and realized they were headed for the mushroom waterfall.

"Butch says its temperature is far colder. But there are some advantages to it that the warm water can't provide."

The noise of the falling water became loud enough she anticipated its touch, but the cold and pummeling impact still made her gasp as he eased her feet beneath the flow. She writhed, her nipples becoming even tighter points as gooseflesh swept her upper torso. Brian kept moving her forward, so water pattered up her shins, her knees, her thighs. The beating rhythm was strong, inexorable. Then he adjusted her so that pounding cold water was on her exposed cunt, her swollen clit.

"Oh…oh." She bucked and shuddered while her Master's avid eyes watched her body strain against the Velcro straps. The raft's water bed movement gave her an erratic rhythm that made the impact of the water against her genitals torment and pleasure both, a climax building and yet held out of reach.

"Lord Brian, you look as if you require assistance."

Butch had appeared above her head, and those gray eyes were covering every inch of her exposed skin, the responses of her body, feeding on them in that way that vampires did, with total absorption. With the right set of vampires, and her Master firmly in control, being viewed this way brought her a surge of additional pleasure.

At Brian's gracious nod, the Texas overlord steadied the raft, freeing both of Brian's hands. Her Master cupped her breasts, his body pushing down on the inflatable enough to tilt her in his direction. His heated mouth closed on her cold nipple, worrying it with heated tongue and lips.

She cried out at the sensation, convulsing under the water's flow. More hands closed around her calves and ankles, and she felt other mouths on her there. The tender crease between her toes and the ball of her foot, her ankles…the insides of her spread knees.

She was too disoriented with lust to lift her head, look through the waterfall and see who was responsible, but there were at least two men down there touching her, caressing her. Possibly Dix, Butch's servant, and maybe one of the other vampires, since she sensed the restrained strength vampires usually exercised to avoid crushing bone.

Brian dipped under the raft, came up on the other side. Slicking back his hair, streams of water etching his shoulders and chest, he bent to attend to her other breast.

"Oh God…" It was impossible to come, the raft having too much random movement, but the water beating on her clit and labia kept pushing her toward that pinnacle. She saw Tucker and Aila sitting on the concrete lip of the lazy river, eyes intent on her helpless thrashings.

Brian took his time with her breast, indulging his own pleasure until she was mindless, almost savage. When he gripped the side of her face, thumb passing over her lips, she bit. He pushed further into her mouth so she was sucking it frantically as his lips and tongue kept lashing at her nipples, the heat at odds with the cold of the falling water.

When she was practically screaming with the constant barrage of sensation, she was moved further forward, so the curtain of water was falling on her abdomen. Another heated mouth closed over her cunt. She shrieked. Her Master straightened then, his hand sliding down over her neck, fingers tangling with the only thing she was wearing. His necklace, the signet ring catching on his thumb as his other fingers closed on her throat, reminding her she had to have his permission.

"Master, please…"

"Do you wish to come for me?"

"Yes." She wailed it.

"Then please me. Wait until I say you can."

Oh God. Whoever was working behind that curtain knew what they were doing. With her legs bound she couldn't stop the sensations from overtaking her. She held his gaze though, put everything she needed and wanted to give to him in it. The fire and hunger in his gaze almost consumed her.

"Now," he said.

The climax hit her like a wall of water ten times as forceful as this one, especially when he bent and sank his fangs into her breast. She bowed up, seeing Butch's lust-fired gaze, feeling his fingers tangled in her hair, holding her head still as Brian took blood from her breast, as her cunt pulsed and gushed with her climax, as she screamed with the force of all of it, sending echoes throughout the pool area.

The waves kept coming and coming, a mix of their sexual talents and the stamina she had as a third mark. All proof of just how truly helpless she was in her binding to him. A binding she never wanted removed.

Brian lifted his head, sealed blood-tinged lips over hers, letting her taste the blood with which she nourished him. Which strengthened the bond all the more. She whimpered into his mouth, pleaded for God knew what, as aftershocks as violent as climaxes shook her.

He lifted his head, traced her face, watched every reaction, drinking it all in as his due. "You want more, need more. Insatiable sweet girl. My servant."

She nodded, panting, wide-eyed, pleading. Brian straightened, looking toward Butch. "I think she has far more to give us. Wouldn't you agree, my lord?"

She had few brain cells left, but enough to know the formality had been intentional. Brian hadn't rejected the tradition of what might be due to their host. He'd only retained the right to make the decision, limiting her access to those who would care for her, ensure her pleasure was part of the equation.

Butch inclined his head. "I think she might at that. Dix?"

Dix came through the curtain of water. His spiky hair was so short that even wet it stood up, but she liked the way the water made the color gleam, and how drops rolled down the angular planes of his sun-browned face. She wanted to touch, to lick. Brian was right. She was all mindless sensuality now, his creature to offer and serve pleasure. Her gaze sought Brian, that connection to her Master. Though he didn't look at her, he felt her regard, answered it.

Watching you serve at my command is something I plan never to deprive myself of again.

God, a threat had never sounded so wonderful.

Butch directed Dix to change places with him, hold the raft while he shifted out of the way. "I think Lord Brian wants you to suckle his servant's breasts and get her ready for his cock again."

"With pleasure."

That was only part of the equation, though. When Dix bent over her face to put his mouth between her breasts, nuzzling his way up the rise toward a nipple, it brought him close to her as well. She could reach his elbow and part of his forearm where her wrist was bound, so she curled her fingers over him, lifted her head to lick his sternum, reach his nipple with her mouth. The nub was beaded with water. As she sucked and licked at it, he nipped hers in response, but she also felt his breath catch. She was giving him pleasure.

Watching them was inspiring the vampires to take a more active role themselves. When Dix clutched the raft by her shoulders, the jolt of his body, the resulting rock of it against the inflatable, told her he was being fucked as he did his Master's bidding. From the mingling of scents, she could tell it was Butch. A flick of her gaze showed Butch's fingers curved tight over Dix's shoulders, holding him steady as he worked his cock into his servant.

Most servants lubricated themselves well for such gatherings, both males and females. Dix's grunt against her flesh said that his Master was a challenging size, even with the right preparation. But all servants knew some types of discomfort only fueled pleasure. When his nipping and licking became less focused, more frantic and sharp, desire unfolded in her once more, stoked by the sexual energy swirling around them.

Another pair of hands had locked onto her ankles, a mouth teasing and sucking on the network of fragile bones. However, the rhythm and vibration of movement from behind that curtain of water told her whatever servant had been ordered to put his mouth on her there was being fucked as well. It had to be the sous chef, which meant the big Viking, Balen, was taking his pleasure. Tucker was still watching poolside, his blue eyes sharp and measuring. He seemed to be the dominant vampire of the pairing, Balen and Reed performing for him.

Her Master's hands slid down her waist, her thighs. Through glazed eyes, she saw him cut through the waterfall, and then he bent to put his mouth where Dix's had been. Any hope at deductive reasoning flew away, her arousal spiking high once more as he lapped between her legs, making her shudder and moan again.

She'd been placed in the center of a clock she suspected was going to see a lot of rotations before dawn called the vampires to bed. And while she trembled at the idea of all those demands, the memory of her Master's beautiful hazel eyes and the solid touch of his hands, the caress of his mouth, said it would all be at his behest, his direction. He'd watch over her every step of the way, even while using her pleasure for his own, pushing her past exhaustion. And then he'd carry her to bed and start all over again.

She was moving again, through the waterfall. She closed her eyes, prepared for the waterfall to pass over her face, but Dix leaned over her, the width of his chest providing that shelter until they were through and he could straighten again. His Master had obviously pulled out to allow for the transport, and Balen and Reed had withdrawn as well.

When they floated into the main pool, her Master was once again directing the raft, though Butch and Dix were still with them. She couldn't see the others, but all she wanted to look at was Brian. Her restraints gave her enough of a reach she could stroke his knuckles where his hand was placed on the raft. His fingers curled over hers, stroking her back.

As they reached the wall, Butch heaved himself out with an impressive ripple of muscle from shoulders to thighs. Dripping wet and magnificent, thick cock erect, he reached down to clasp Dix's hand and pulled him out one-armed, pushing him immediately toward a solid-looking wooden chair.

"Grab the arms. You're going to need the brace."

Dix had barely a second to bend over the chair and comply before Butch shoved his cock into his narrow ass again. Watching two men fuck had an undeniably erotic savagery to it that claimed her attention, kept her libido simmering.

Keep watching them. I'm going to watch you, while Tia and Aila enjoy your taste.

Her thigh muscles tightened as a female mouth closed over her cunt, tasting and suckling. Aila, because Tia stood at her hip, looking at Debra like a rare treat. Brian hiked himself up onto the wall, sitting where she could see him. He was no less magnificent than Butch. She wanted to suckle every bead of water off him, put her mouth over his cock, standing proud and thick between his thighs. She wanted to watch him watching her.

I gave you an order. You watch Butch and Dix. You don't have permission to look at me.

She felt the denial of that keenly, but watching Butch and Dix only made her blood heat further, her body start gathering for another climax under Aila's clever mouth. God, Butch was strong, even for a vampire. He caught Dix by his nape, pushed him down on a mat on all fours. Dix braced himself, grunting while Butch's hips pistoned. Then his Master was gripping Dix's throat, bringing him up to band an arm around his chest as he thrust even harder. Dix's body arched, his cock jutting out, unrelieved. Reed knelt in front of him, closing his mouth on Dix's organ as Balen pushed him down, worked his cock into his own servant's backside.

"Not until I come, you horny bastard," Butch muttered in his servant's ear.

"Then get on with it already," Dix gasped. Butch gave a nasty laugh, reaching down to grasp his servant's testicles in a fist that constricted, made Dix curse.

Debra moaned at all the stimulation. The female servant was working her pussy with soft lips, clever flicks of her tongue. Her Mistress leaned over Debra, pinched her nipples, making her arch and gasp. God, she was going to go over again.

Yes. You are. Now.

And she did, responding to her Master's demand, gushing against another mouth while he watched with endless appreciation.

§

By the time the evening was drawing to a close, she'd lost track of how many times she'd come, how many times she'd inspired others to do so. She'd been kept on the raft, where she experienced a wealth of heated mouths and exploring fingers. She was also taken back to the pummeling pleasures of the waterfall once or twice. With her attached to the inflatable, the vampires considered her part of the water toy offerings. One that inspired them to enjoy their own servants just as intensely, the stimulating result of her Master generously allowing them to touch, kiss, suckle and watch her build to a pinnacle to send her over, again and again.

Sex with the other servants or vampires was not part of the equation. Brian had drawn a line with Graham and held it. Yet though most of the vampires fucked their own servants during the course of the evening—Butch took Dix at least three times—Brian didn't avail himself of his own servant the same way. It didn't take long for her to notice and then recognize it as an intentional torment.

To make it worse, he stayed close to her throughout everything, touched her constantly. When she was screaming out her next waterfall climax, her fingers were digging into his forearms as he held her wrists, reinforcing the Velcro straps. He bent and captured her mouth, teasing her lips and tongue with his own. When Tia was trying out the waterproof dual-headed vibrator on her, he cupped her breasts, pinching her nipples with greater and greater force as the dildos were worked in and out of her anus and pussy. Reed and Aila freed her ankles for that and held her knees folded against her abdomen, making the sensations even more excruciating.

She needed him to claim her, fuck her hard and endlessly. She'd reached an advanced state of disorientation, a deprivation-induced subspace, where it was all she could think about. When he finally bid the others good night, she was in a daze of want and exhaustion. Her gaze clung to him as he tucked a short towel around his waist, his only nod to modesty before he gestured to her to follow him out of the pool area.

She stumbled over the threshold from the patio to the dining room. But when she did, he was there, arm around her waist. He swung her up into his arms, carrying her.

I'm sorry.

"I'll tell you when to be sorry, Debra. Until then, I don't want to hear another apology from you."

His voice was a sensual growl. Once he reached the guestroom, he closed the door and took her to the bed, laid her down on her back. He shed the towel from his hips, and her eyes latched onto his cock, more than ready to do as she desired.

Whose desires are important, Debra?

"Yours, Master," she whispered. But she might die if he didn't take her.

He put a knee on the bed between her legs, which had automatically spread for her Master. He saw it, his lips tightening, but he bent and kissed her navel, held his lips there. Despite her urgent pulse of need, the protracted moment penetrated her mind, roused other needs. Her heart rate slowed to a thud, her throat thickening. She didn't want him inside her merely to fulfill a primal need for fucking. It was to feel complete, every part of her locked with him, mind, body and soul. She touched the strands of hair across his brow with quivering fingers, and he lifted his head.

Bliss. He slid up her body, bracing his hands on either side of her shoulders as she looked up at him, continuing to thread her trembling fingers through his hair. Her body felt weak, pliable, even as what pounded inside her heart was as powerful as crashing waves.

"I love you," she said.

She'd thought it so often these past few years but hadn't said it, kept it tucked in her mind. His eyes glittered like starlight. She tried to smile but couldn't. He didn't smile either. Instead, he came down, put his body on hers. Pressed his elbows on either side of her shoulders, cradled her face in his hands and, with a shift of his hips, slowly pushed his cock inside of her.

Intense sensation rolled through her, somewhere between an aftershock and climax, all the pent up need and desire she'd felt these many hours. She clung to his waist, fingers digging into the rise of his buttocks, her hips lifting to take him deeper. Her legs locked over her forearms, wanting to hold him even tighter, keep him lodged within her forever. As his weight pushed her deeper into the mattress, she felt the pressure of the covers against her third mark, the crossed sword image. She was marked as his family. As his, period.

The sound that came from her throat was relief, need, want, love. It was the crowning victory of the night, the physical symbolism reflecting the emotional. At last he'd filled her, connected with her, joined with her in a way that felt like the link was permanent, not just when their flesh was joined. She wouldn't wake up and find this had all been a dream.

His declaration before the others had been what she'd needed. From that moment forward, she'd felt no trepidation serving the others, because he'd truly been *with* her. She could even have handled Graham.

You'll never need to handle someone like Graham. I won't permit anyone to abuse my servant. Ever.

His eyes glittered with that perilous edge that made her breath catch. As if she needed anything else to make her heart pound harder. Tonight she'd been the type of servant she'd hoped she could be for him. All she'd needed was...

Me to be the type of Master worth such service. You had to trust me, believe in me.

He pushed deeper into her and she let out a soft moan, making his expression warm with lust and love both. "But you're wrong," he said, holding her gaze. "You made the first step with Jia-Li, even before I confronted Graham. You're one of the bravest women I know." He slid his lips beneath her ear, along her throat. As his fangs pierced her there, she closed her eyes, shuddered. When he slid his arms beneath her, wrapping her up in his strength, she shifted her grip to band around his shoulders and waist, hold him.

Several more thrusts, their bodies rocking together. She could feel the response he'd controlled all night gathering. It had kept his cock a mouthwatering size that her pussy contracted around now, milking him, drawing him out. His buttocks and thigh muscles steeled to climactic rigidity, his breath rasping, eyes flashing hazel fire as his mouth became taut.

"Yes, please..." She whispered it, and her Master granted her wish.

He began to release, his seed jetting inside her. A cry tore from her throat. Remarkably, another intense orgasm gripped her, provoked by how his marking felt, inside and out. He let out a reverent curse, pushing up to thrust even harder into her, now holding nothing back. She tore furrows in his his back, her hips lifting, meeting him on every impact, her chin lifting to expose her throat, offering him everything.

Life, heart, soul, mind. Everything she was.

She wasn't sure if time didn't completely stop, because she didn't remember how it ended. Just eventually, slowly, she became aware of them in the bed again, instead of floating, spinning in some eternal either where it was just the two of them and endless pleasure. He let himself lay down on her, one arm around her back, the other bracing himself so his full weight wasn't on her. His breath rasped against her ear, his hair brushed her face. Their limbs were still twined together, their bodies still joined.

Inseparable.

Master and servant.

Chapter Nine

Two days later, they were home again. Brian wanted her to stay with him that first dawn, and she was happy to do so, woken at dusk by him kissing his way down her body, then coming back to join them, take them both on a slide to a shuddering, quiet climax. Afterward, as he held her, stroking her hair, she could feel the weight of his thoughts, though his mind wasn't available to her as it had been that brief, unforgettable time at Butch's. Vampires didn't typically keep their minds open that way to their servants. She hadn't expected it to be more than a temporary, amazing gift. But that rational thought didn't prevent worry from creeping back into her mind.

Yes, some of the changes to their relationship had started to happen before they left for Texas, but sometimes when getting back into the same routine, things could return to same old, same old. It could have been just an interlude...

"At a certain point, you stop testing a theory and consider it proven." He spoke quietly against her hair. "I expect my behavior of the past few years deserves a fair amount of testing, but I can assure you the past week wasn't just an interlude, Debra."

She nodded against his chest. "Yes, my lord."

He sighed, rolled her over and pinned her, framing her face in his hands. "We're both scientific people. We analyze too much, downplay emotions and try to be rational about everything." His gaze held her. "You've gotten in the habit of beating down your emotions to make things bearable for you, easier for me. You decided that was the best course to take. It's not any more. I want the scientist, but I also want the woman who loves and feels. Don't hold that back from me."

She swallowed. "I know. But for so long, I thought loving you made me have unrealistic expectations of your feelings. It's hard to get past that."

"Just because your Master is a clueless idiot is no reason for you to cater to it." He allowed himself a serious smile, touched her face. "It's not unrealistic to expect my love in exchange for your exceptional loyalty, devotion and unconditional service. Help the scientist in me remember that I am man and Master. The man who loves you back."

As he settled beside her, began stroking her hair again, she considered that. Drew equations on his chest. "You asked me why I made the choice I did," she said slowly. "It was based on a faulty hypothesis."

His fingers stilled. "Oh?"

She smiled against his chest, though it was a painful one. This hadn't been an easy journey, for all that it was the most worthwhile one she'd taken in her life. "I thought, 'if I serve him well enough, then he will be everything I hope he is.'"

Every fluffy woman's magazine in the world would have jumped on that for the horrible mistake it was. A woman couldn't change a man's heart, his mind. Only he could do that. She was an intelligent woman, had known it. But she couldn't follow her thoughts. She'd followed her heart, because her feelings had been so irrefutable. A way she'd never felt before.

"You've always put a woman's intuition into your science, and I've never known it to fail. It didn't this time. Despite my best efforts."

Another painful smile. He found it with sensitive fingertips, traced her mouth, his knuckle giving her cheek a light brush before he rested the hand on her hip. She listened to his heart beat beneath her ear, thought some more. She wrote some more random equations on his chest before she spoke again. "So what were you thinking about?"

"Your grandfather," Brian answered, surprising her. "What you told him, about me not looking like a scientist."

He was silent a moment, as if pondering the wisdom of what he was about to say. Then he sighed, gave a self-deprecating laugh, an unusual sound that had her glancing up at his brooding face. "But I am, Debra," he said, meeting her gaze squarely. "While I'm hunched over my laptop, studying tissue samples or running data, I'm rubbing shoulders with vampires who are at the top of the food chain, who fight formidable opponents hand to hand and walk away victorious. Beyond the other reasons I've given you, it's made me wonder, more than once, if you regretted your choice to me. That was why I was jealous of Jacob."

Shock filled her. He seemed relieved to see it, which shocked her further. He pressed a kiss to her temple. Then he nudged her to her back again, putting himself between her willing thighs. As he seated himself between them, her eyes widened at the probe of his stiff cock. The recovery time was exceptional, even for him.

"I plan to be a great deal more demanding with my servant than I have been in the past. Another reason I expect her to get at least three hours of sleep a day." He gave her a stern look, then sobered. She stilled, her lips parting as he eased into her, inexorable in his demand, but being slow and gentle about it all the same. He'd used her hard the past couple of nights, enough she'd felt the effects of it during her work day. She loved it. From the satisfied gleam in his eye, she thought he did as well.

"I don't think of any female but you, Debra. Not since the day I met you."

She drew in a breath as he pushed into her, then withdrew until he stroked her opening with the head of his cock. Then he pushed in again, wresting a moan from her throat as he lodged deep and stilled. His hazel eyes were intent, vibrant.

"Though it doesn't come out sounding complimentary in any way, even that night, with Lady Carmela, was about you. In a terrible way I will never repeat."

At the twist in her heart, he stroked her temples, drawing her eyes back to him again. "I promise," he said.

She gave a quick nod, overwhelmed with feeling. The memory still hurt, but she knew now it would heal, everything they did together from here forward a balm that would turn a wound into a scar, a lesson that had brought them both to this moment. This indescribable moment.

His face reflected an intent Master's pleasure at her reaction. "I've never needed any woman for my pleasure but you, Debra. And when I wish to share my mind, my discoveries, I think of you."

He continued to thrust, forward and back. Her pulse was elevating and he saw it, dipping his head to suck on the artery. She felt the scrape of his fangs as she tilted back her head, asking for that penetration instinctively. His thumb slid along the pounding track.

"I can watch you stare into a microscope, your brow furrowing, the way you press your lips together when you're concentrating, and suddenly I want you under me like this. I want to see that same focus when I bring your climax upon you and make you lose control. It's a deep pleasure to me, watching you surrender yourself to me fully..."

He shoved in hard then, wresting a full throated cry from her. He tangled her hair around his fist, pulled on her scalp as she held his gaze.

"There is no other female I desire, Debra. Do you understand?"

"Yes. Yes, Master. Oh…"

The words branded themselves inside her as the climax overtook her. She held onto him, rode that wild tide safely in his arms, and tightened her grip as he joined her in the churning, pleasurable joy of coming in to shore together.

Usually when a scientist reached the conclusion she most wanted to hear, she did further testing to ensure she wasn't biasing the experiment with her own needs. But maybe when it came to the human heart, a different method made more sense. Where science was replaced with faith.

In the end, her hypothesis had been based not on science or if/then statements, but on the belief that when all the debris was cleared away, she'd find the man who loved her as much as she loved him.

Thank God, she'd been right.

Epilogue

Brian strode down the hallway, his head down as he considered the latest statistics from the Texas visit. He needed several more test subjects. Debra had collected a list of candidates, one of them in Iceland. He'd never been to Iceland, and wondered at the kind of vampire who would choose to settle in such cold. Of course, there was protracted darkness there...

Though there were ethical questions to resolve, what they needed was data on unstable made vampires. Which meant he needed several brought to the lab before they were executed, so he could get live tissue samples, interview them like he had Butch. He didn't relish such unpleasantness, but that was where a scientist's detachment was necessary. Their end would be humane and they would be in a contained, safe environment until that time. He could justify his need with that. It would still be damned uncomfortable, but the whole point of all this was to cut down on the number of made vampires necessitating execution in the future.

Sensing something amiss, he stopped. Jacob stood just past him on the left side of the hall, watching him with an amused look. The servant had obviously moved out of his way rather than be plowed over. "Good thing it wasn't my Mistress again," he said. "She'd have strapped you down and used you as a carpet runner for a week to reinforce the lesson."

"I'm sure you would have gone out and stepped in dog shit just for the pleasure of tracking it across my body."

"My lord, I hadn't thought of it. But thank you for planting the suggestion." Jacob grinned, but then a more serious look came to his eye. "My lady has a friendship with Butch Dorn. He called and gave a detailed account of your visit last week."

"Yes, it was productive. I think the data will be useful."

"I expect it will."

From the spark in Jacob's blue eyes, Brian wondered what Butch had shared during that phone conversation. God knew he'd made some pretty bold assumptions that night which might or might not be supported by Lady Lyssa. As Graham had guessed, he'd bluffed.

With great determination.

Brian braced himself, but Jacob merely nodded and resumed his course. After a thoughtful moment, Brian did the same. He'd almost reached the opposite end of the corridor before he heard the servant call to him again.

"My lord?"

Brian glanced back at him. Jacob cocked his head. "Going toe-to-toe with a vampire four times your age, you won't be called a nerd anymore. Except by Gideon."

"One day I will put *his* head through a wall," Brian retorted. "Right next to yours."

"My lady is far more likely to do that first." Jacob flashed a grin. "Give my regards to Debra. I saw her yesterday and she looked happier than I've ever seen her. No doubt because she's back here, where I can bring her cookies."

"Keep your cookies to yourself," Brian advised, and Jacob's grin grew wider. The servant turned, headed up the hallway once more.

"She likes sugar cookies best," he called over his shoulder. "The cook just made a fresh batch. Maybe you could swing by there on the way to the lab."

Brian shook his head, but he only took two steps toward his original destination before he changed direction toward the kitchen. He was already anticipating Debra taking pieces of that cookie from his fingers, kissing lips frosted with sugar...

His servant had brought sweetness to his life in ways he hadn't anticipated. He fully intended to return the favor.

Sample Excerpt

Like Joey W. Hill's vampire world? Here's a taste of the first book of the Vampire Queen series, *The Vampire Queen's Servant* (Jacob and Lyssa's story):

Lyssa wanted a meal. Preferably something muscular, a man whose long, powerful body would serve her well as she took his blood. She would hold him down, drink her fill and ride him hard. Take him deep, making him give up his rich blood and hot seed to her body at the same time. She'd push him to exhaustion, beyond rational thought. All those wonderful muscles would be taut and slick as he pounded into her with single-minded urgency, his most primitive instincts making him into a fierce, beautiful rutting animal.

Just imagining it made heat shimmer over her skin. As she gazed out the window from the shadows of the backseat of her limo, her lips parted, her tongue caressing the backside of her fangs as if she could already taste him.

For months she'd made herself take blood functionally, letting it nourish her the way freeze-dried packets would keep a lost camper alive. But like most vampires, her desire for blood was intertwined with her need to dominate her victim sexually. Without that, the blood had no taste. No vitality.

She missed taking alpha males. She enjoyed the fight, their resistance, the sweet taste of heated blood. The perception, if only for a moment, that the hunt would be a challenge. A vampire didn't survive by being ruled by her compulsions, any more than a woman survived by being consumed by her most private desires. But tonight she needed release, and she was feeling reckless enough not to care about the consequences to her fragile heart.

Her nails were just the beginning. A manicure, then a man.

It irritated her that the car in the deserted parking lot of the salon was not Max's. Maybe her manicurist had experienced car trouble and borrowed someone else's vehicle. Still, it set off alarm bells in Lyssa's head. But since her limo was an evening's rental while she stayed in Atlanta, she couldn't very well ask the driver to scope out the area for signs of rival vampires. Of course, if she'd had a marked human servant, he could have performed the task for her.

She studied her nails by the light thrown into the car from the parking lot lamps. Hellhound that he was, her Irish wolfhound Bran had torn one when she was indulging his incessant need for attention. It had grown back to the half-inch length she preferred in no time, but the glossy burgundy polish could not be regenerated. Perfection was essential, particularly these days when showing any vulnerability could create dangerous situations. Though she easily could afford to pay a manicurist to come to her home, her enemies needed to know she wouldn't hesitate to go out to seek simple indulgences.

The hell with it. So it wasn't Max's car. If it was a trap or trick, she was ready to prove to any enemy or potential suitor foolish enough to challenge her she was not to be trifled with – particularly not when she teetered on the edge of full blown blood lust.

Read another taste of Jacob and Lyssa's story on The Vampire Queen's Servant page on Joey's website.

http://www.storywitch.com/book-vqs-vqs